LEOPOLDO GOUT

GENIUS
the
revolution

FEIWEL AND FRIENDS
NEW YORK

A FEIWEL AND FRIENDS BOOK

An imprint of Macmillan Publishing Group, LLC

175 Fifth Avenue, New York, NY 10010

Our books may be purchased in bulk for promotional, educational, or business use. Please contact your local bookseller or the Macmillan Corporate and Premium Sales Department at (800) 221-7945 ext. 5442 or by e-mail at MacmillanSpecialMarkets@macmillan.com.

Library of Congress Control Number: 2017956982

ISBN 978-1-250-04583-6 (hardcover) / ISBN 978-1-250-19470-1 (ebook)

Endpaper credits: Eye photographs © JR-ART.net; illustrations © James Manning; brick wall © Shutterstock/Dan Kosmayer

Book design by Liz Dresner and Sophie Erb

Feiwel and Friends logo designed by Filomena Tuosto

First edition, 2018

10 9 8 7 6 5 4 3 2 1

fiercereads.com

To all the DREAMERS:
Stay Strong—light will always splinter the darkness.

ONDSCAN

To all black box lab staffers:
We find ourselves at a turning point.

I have always been honest with you about my goals and my intentions with our work. You were handpicked from, literally, thousands of candidates to join me in changing civilization for the better. We all know how afflicted the world is with suffering, poverty, violence, environmental destruction, and persecution. And we all want to change it—to stop the ills of the world and usher in a new age that we can own.

I promised you that when you joined the brain trust I would do everything in my power to ensure that we were successful. I gave you every tool you could ever need and all the space and encouragement. I provided food, shelter, and every amenity to guarantee your comfort. All I asked in return was for you to abandon all doubt and commit your considerable talents to helping me design a world in which the stagnant, old ways would no longer hold sway over the brilliance of youth.

And you have done magnificent things.

I have been to all of the black box labs and seen your work firsthand. I have witnessed your breakthroughs and championed your failures (because, as we all know, failure is the ultimate teaching tool). Every single day spent in your company has been surprising and revelatory. I believe in you and our mission now more than I ever have before.

That is why I am writing you this message.

As long as there have been dreamers and innovators, there have been those afraid of change and desperate to keep the status quo. For every bright-eyed visionary looking to galvanize new technologies, there are one hundred doomsayers eager to squash her reveries. I am afraid that there are desperate young prodigies who want to stop us from achieving our goals.

Hard to believe, I know. But it's true.

They are the LODGE, and they are out there right now, making contact with our enemies—like Terminal—to find ways to stop us. They will be reaching out to you. Trying to break down our walls. I am asking you to be strong, to stay the course, and to resist their messaging. At the end of the day, I know this is merely a passing storm, one of many we've already weathered.

So hunker down. Lock the doors. Arm the security systems.

Trust no one outside of the lab. Ignore all external e-mails and messages. Do not listen to the media. We need to isolate ourselves and focus our minds. I am available whenever you need me. We are so close.

In six days, Shiva will be ready to launch. The clock starts now.

Yours in solidarity and vision,
Kiran

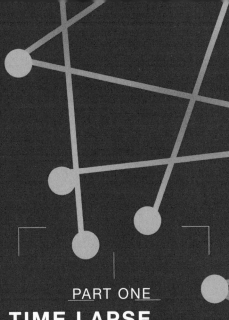

PART ONE
TIME LAPSE

Three hours after we landed in Beijing, I located my father.

He was at the Municipal Number 23 detention center. Thankfully, he hadn't been transferred to a prison yet. No doubt Interpol's involvement in his case kept him from being sent directly to one of the overcrowded jails. Given the seriousness of the charges against him, though, that was likely to change. After the interrogation was finished, the odds were high that he would be sent straight to a maximum-security prison. If that happened, we'd likely never get him out.

Now that we had found him, it was time to do my thing.

The Painted Wolf thing.

Even if my father wasn't in prison, getting him out of a detention center wasn't going to be an easy feat. I'd have to rely on a lot of the same skills I'd used when we busted Rex out in New York but without the advanced gear. I'd have to use the art of talk and bluster.

Pretending to be a lawyer in the States was relatively easy; I used my accent for one. Getting away with something like that in my home country, however, was going to be trickier. I'd played the underground journalist, the stone-faced security agent, and the concerned business partner, but now I needed to create someone new. Someone more believable than all the others combined. This was going to require more research and more time—the one thing we didn't have.

We all rode in a cab together on the way to the detention facility.

I sat up front with the driver, an older man from Nankin, while Rex, Tunde, and Teo squeezed into the backseat. They had their bags piled on their laps and were going through whatever tech they had readily available—cell phones, my pin cameras, scattered surveillance tech like earbud mics and wires.

The second I realized where my father was being held, I bought some new clothes—slacks, a blouse, and sleek shoes. I aged myself up with some subtle makeup effects; I wanted to appear as **professional and intimidating** as possible.

As the cab slowly made its way through the late-afternoon traffic, I went online to figure out my angle. Though the detention center didn't have an active website, several of its employees did. Using their social media accounts—reading up on their colleagues, their families, and their friends—I was able to get a good sense of the corporate structure of the center. I knew the various departments, who was in charge, and was even able to piece together several current schedules. These tiny nuggets of innocuous information were like treasure chests.

Fifteen minutes from our arrival time, I made the first call. Rex had taken a few minutes to spoof my cell number to make it look like I was calling from the discipline commission, several layers of bureaucracy above the jails and prisons. One of the security guards I'd found online answered the call. She was very businesslike.

"This is Liu Xiansheng."

"Good afternoon! I'm Mrs. Huang, the coordinator for the department of facilities management, badge number six-five-two-zero. I'm on my way now and should be there in twenty minutes to do my inspection of the facility."

I could hear Liu Xiansheng swallow hard over the phone.

"I—I don't have this appointment on my calendar—"

"What do you mean?" I asked assertively. "It has been scheduled for weeks. I was told I'd have access to the entire facility. I have a list of prisoners that I'll be meeting with as well as center staff. Are you telling me **you don't know** about this?"

Liu Xiansheng scrambled. "No," she said, "I just—"

"Maybe I should contact your superior to clarify the situation here—"

"Oh look, here it is. Yes. I do have you scheduled," Liu lied. "We will have everything ready for you when you arrive. I will have a list of staff and prisoners available, and you can choose whom you would like to meet with. We look forward to seeing you soon."

"Excellent," I said, then hung up.

I spent most of the rest of the drive online creating a fake ID. A lot of IDs were digital now, and with the right tweaking I knew I could pull off something fairly convincing. In our final few minutes on the road, I refreshed my makeup and pulled back my hair in a tight, professional bun.

Two blocks from the municipal detention center, I had the cab pull over so the boys could get out. I did not get out with them. Teo had already used mapping software to scout out a rooftop on a nearby building where he could provide surveillance, while Rex and Tunde hacked into the detention center's closed-circuit-TV camera system. They had just upgraded to a new wireless system, which meant we could have eyes inside the building as well as outside.

"You guys know the plan?" I asked the boys.

"We're on it," Rex said.

1.1

The cab dropped me off alone, and Liu Xiansheng met me in the lobby.

She was young and full of smiles.

"Your ID, please," she said, her lips barely moving. "And your cell."

I pulled out my cell and showed her the ID. She looked it over, glancing from the screen to my face and back again several times. I was wearing a pair of reading glasses but she didn't bat an eye, which was good, because these reading glasses were outfitted with multiple 360-degree surveillance cameras and spot microphones. (The boys had done some quick tweaks to the frames we'd picked up when I went clothes shopping.) Finally, Liu nodded her approval.

"I'm afraid I will need to keep your cellular phone here," Liu said.

"Of course."

I handed it to her.

It worked. I was in. As Liu went to a desk to grab some paperwork and drop off my cell phone, I whispered to the tiny earpiece I was wearing, hoping Rex would hear me clearly.

"I'm in," I said.

"Looking good," Rex replied. "On your right."

I glanced up at the corner to my right and saw a camera mounted there. I gave a flash of a smile to Rex before Liu returned with a file folder.

Before she could even open her mouth to say a word, I said: "First, I'm going to need to interview several of the prisoners, then the staff, and finally I'll need a tour of the premises so I can confirm my findings for myself."

Nodding, Liu handed me a list of men at the detention center.

I scanned it and pointed to three names. My father's was first.

Liu looked at the sheet and nodded in agreement.

"Right this way, please," she said.

I walked down the corridor, flanked by Liu and two armed guards. None of them seemed particularly suspicious. If anything, they acted as though this was just another visit, just another part of a long day. That gave me some confidence, but I also knew things could change in a matter of microseconds. One false word, one misstep, and they wouldn't hesitate to toss me into a cell alongside my father.

I needed to be **focused.**

"I'm almost in the room," I whispered.

Rex said, through the earpiece: "I can see your dad on the CCTV cameras. He's sitting at the back of the room. There is one guard in the room with him."

I let the conference room door close behind me as I stepped inside. The room was large—there were four tables, empty save for one. My father sat there, arms on the tabletop in front of him. A guard stood on the opposite side of the room, eyeing me coldly. I crossed the room slowly, confidently.

My heart was racing so fast I worried it would bruise my ribs.

Reaching the back of the room, I sat down across from my father. He looked exhausted. Not just from sleep deprivation but from emotional fatigue as well. The crimes my father was charged with carried **serious weight**, and there were so many people—Chinese authorities, Interpol, FBI, and Mossad—who wanted answers. Answers that my father didn't have.

Just like in Nigeria, my father recognized me right away. I didn't have to say a word, didn't even remove my glasses. He leaned forward and rested his elbows on the table. I could hear his shackles clank under the table and my heart sank. The thought of my father in chains, it was nearly too much to bear.

"Hello," I said as Liu and the guards walked away. "My name is Mrs. Huang. I'm with the department of facilities management. I'd like to ask you a few questions about your time here at the detention center."

The door closed behind me. Liu and the guards were gone, and as soon as they were out of earshot, my father leaned in, his eyes wide.

"Cai," my father whispered, "what are you doing?"

"I'm here to get you out."

"There are cameras on every wall," my father said.

"We're in control of the cameras. The plan is simple. I'm going to interview you and you're going to complain and then I'll act very upset. I'll tell the woman from the office here that I need to speak to management, that you've been mistreated and need to be moved to a hospital. We'll have an ambulance come, and security at the hospital will be much lighter. That's the first part. Second—"

My father shook his head. "I'm sorry, Cai. It will not work."

"Why? It seems like it will work just fine. I've done this before."

My father raised an eyebrow at that.

"Well," I said, "I mean I've done . . . Look, it doesn't matter. We have to get you out of here and this is our only chance, okay?"

My father spoke urgently. "They are expecting you."

I stopped breathing for a second.

In my earpiece, Rex said, "Hang on, what did he just say?"

"They've been asking me about a team of young people," my father continued. "A Mexican or American boy, a Nigerian boy, and a Chinese girl. After meeting your American and Nigerian friends last week, I knew the Chinese girl was you."

Interview with Cai's father

In my earpiece, Rex said, "Cai, you need to get out now. . . ."

"Who were these people?" I asked my father.

He shook his head. "I don't know, but I do know that they'll be watching me here. If you try to remove me, they'll hear about it and things will only get worse. They're using me as a pawn. I can't leave here unless the charges are dropped."

I drew in a deep breath, mind racing, searching for any way to make our original plan work. But my father was right. Without knowing who was watching us, any action could just make things worse. Reluctantly, I nodded to him.

"I will get you out of here, Father. Count on it."

Then, into my earpiece, I said, "Rex, go ahead and restart the cameras and **make the call** in about thirty seconds."

I stood and thanked my father as professionally as I could. Even with my stomach doing somersaults and my eyes threatening to tear up, I kept my composure. The guards stepped into the room the moment I stood; one held the door open for me as I crossed the vast expanse of dull gray carpet as slowly as I could. I needed to give Rex time to make his call.

Sure enough, it worked.

Liu appeared in the doorway, looking quite concerned.

"I just received an important call," she said. "You are to call Deputy Minister Yang immediately. Here is your phone back."

Liu handed me my cell. I dialed up Rex and tried to act as serious and concerned as possible as he said, "We're packing up. See you down on the street in a few minutes." I hung up my cell and pocketed it.

"Unfortunately, there has been an emergency," I told Liu. "I'll have to reschedule the rest of the inspection. I'm not convinced that this facility is meeting every standard. I will be coming back. Soon."

As I walked out of the building, Rex whispered into my earpiece.

"Damn, that was cold," he said.

"I need them to take care of my father," I replied as I walked through the front gates of the detention center to the street. "And **I'm not going to give up.**"

1.2

Tunde, Teo, and Rex had a cab pick me up in front of the detention center.

It took me a few blocks away where they were waiting.

Each of them had a duffel bag tossed over their shoulders, loaded high with gear, and we walked as quickly as possible through the crowds that frequented the markets at the end of Tiantan East Road. As we walked, Tunde seemed distracted, staring off into the crowds as though he was looking for something or someone in particular. He paused several times.

"What's up?" I asked him as we rounded a corner.

"It just looked like there were some people following us."

"Who?" I glanced into the throng behind us.

"A group of young people. Maybe I am mistaken," Tunde said.

I took Tunde's hunch seriously and stealthily glanced around. The streets were incredibly crowded. A storm was about to break overhead, and all of the pedestrians were trying to get their shopping done before the downpour. I didn't see anyone unusual in the crowd; most of the people milling about appeared to be tourists.

"I don't see anyone," I told Tunde.

"Perhaps I was mistaken," he replied.

"So," Rex asked me, getting back to plans, "what're you thinking?"

"There's a microblogger I've worked with in the past. She's got some insane deep-web connections and owes me a few favors. I don't want to pull her into anything too dangerous, but she might be able to find a way to get my father's record **wiped clean**. What do you guys think?"

We pushed through the shoppers, past men hawking umbrellas and women pushing carts filled with fruits and vegetables. I noticed a stand of spices like fennel and star anise and thought about my mother. I wanted desperately to call her and check in but knew I couldn't.

Beijing

Teo was first to answer. "Sounds risky. How can we trust her?"

"She's a friend."

Teo shrugged. "I have a lot of friends. I don't trust any of them."

Rex said, "Well, maybe that's 'cause of your bad attitude."

"I trust her," I said. "That should be enough."

"And I trust whoever Cai trusts," Tunde added.

"That's good and all," Teo said. "But every time we reach out, every time we make a connection, that links us to other people—people who we might endanger or who could endanger us. I didn't spend the last few years living under a rock just to have everything **blow up** in my face now."

"Cai knows what she's doing," Rex said. "Cai is the smartest, most selfless person I've ever met," he continued, pulling Teo to the side. "We wouldn't be here if it weren't for her. Truth is, Cai's the only one who can stop Kiran. You've been trying for years. . . . It's time to let someone else take charge. Cai can do it."

I wanted to hug him then and there, but it started to pour.

I motioned for everyone to follow me down a narrow alleyway between two gaudily lit cell phone stores. In Beijing, cell phone stores are nearly as common as noodle houses. We stopped beneath an awning to get out of the rain.

"I'll be back in two minutes," I told the guys.

Darting into one of the cell phone stores, I asked the young woman with spiky hair working the counter for a cheap, prepaid cell. Nothing smart. Nothing touch-screen. She handed me a Nokia knockoff the size of a small notebook. It came with an access code she scribbled out on a piece of paper and enough minutes to make a quick call. I paid and made my way back to the boys.

"My friend is called Rodger Dodger. She's somewhat of an activist, somewhat of a journalist. What she does is very dangerous. I can't guarantee she'll be willing to help us out, but she's helped me before."

Teo narrowed his eyes, suspicious.

"I need you to trust me on this," I told him.

Rex elbowed his brother.

"Fine," Teo said. "Make the call."

Getting to Rodger Dodger meant calling through a series of numbers. She'd cloaked her location through a Beijing bank that instantly forwarded the call to a bakery in Nanjing that pushed the call through a call center in Suzhou before a young man's voice answered the phone in English. "Hello?"

"Painted Wolf calling for Rodger Dodger," I said.

"One second."

There was a series of clicks before the line picked up again. I realized at that moment that I'd never actually talked to Rodger Dodger. All of our communication had been by text or encrypted e-mail. I knew a few vague details about her—young, female, educated—but could not put a face or a voice to the name. And it was an odd name. Where on Earth would she have come up with Rodger Dodger?

"Painted Wolf," she said. "You're back in China."

"Yes," I said, "and I need some help."

"I noticed a lot of chatter on the feeds. Someone picked up a still of you on the street in Beijing earlier today; lot of rumors going around. Hope you're keeping your head low like usual."

"I'm trying," I said, "but it's not easy."

"Tell me about it. So what do you need?"

"Can't say over the phone. Any chance we can meet?"

"Sure," Rodger Dodger said. "There's a dumpling place a few blocks east of where you're standing right now. I'll meet you there in an hour."

I couldn't help but look out, past Rex, Teo, and Tunde, into the crowds passing by. Even though I knew Rodger Dodger had likely just pinpointed my location using pings from a cell tower or some sort of **tracking program** via the line, there was something spooky about the fact that she knew exactly where I was.

"Okay," I said. "See you then."

I hung up and pulled the cell's SIM card.

Then I crushed it under my shoe before tossing the cell into a storm drain.

"So," I asked the boys, "who's up for dumplings?"

2. Rex

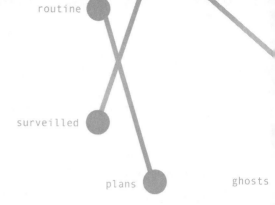

6 DAYS UNTIL SHIVA

If Kolkata seemed crazy crowded, Beijing had it beat.

I was thankful I wasn't attempting to navigate the city alone, but, regardless, the experience was a blur of neon lights, rain, steam, and glass and steel.

I won't lie: I loved every minute of it.

That sounds strange, considering the pressure we were under. But at that point I'd gotten used to it. Being on the run, chased across continents, stressed that every hour might be your last moment before a life behind bars, had become familiar. Routine even.

That's crazy to say.

But it's true.

I will say that it wasn't the adrenaline surge of constantly being on the verge of being arrested that I loved but the fact that I was with family. Having my best friends at my side made me feel secure, and having Teo right there next to me made me confident. Even with the crowds and the rain beating down on my head, I felt stronger than I had in weeks.

Call it the big brother phenomenon.

Ever since I was little, I'd looked up to Teo. I'd turned to him for the answers that Papa or Ma couldn't give me. Usually, he had them. When some kid at school gave me a hard time, Teo always offered to "talk" to the bully. He could see I was upset even before I'd registered the emotion. He was there when I felt lonely.

That's probably why his disappearance hurt so much.

That's certainly why having him back felt so good.

Still, I knew getting into the groove again wasn't going to be easy.

Teo hadn't exactly offered up every detail on what he'd done while he was gone, but whatever it was had made his rough edges that much sharper. Perhaps it was just stress, but he definitely had a shorter fuse.

And I wasn't going to tolerate him taking it out on Cai.

The fact that he doubted her was one thing. Considering what Teo had been involved in over the last couple years, I didn't expect him to go along with all of our plans right away. It was the way he did it that got to me.

As we followed Cai to the dumpling place, navigating a warren of wet side streets, my brother walked slower than the rest of us.

I dropped back beside him.

Something had his hackles up.

"Why're you acting like this?" I asked him.

"We're in China, Rex. This is the most surveilled state in the world. Everything we do here is recorded. Maybe there isn't someone watching the footage as we speak, but our being ghosts isn't going to last very long."

"Cai is the real deal. She lives here. This is her playground."

"And her little friend? I still don't trust her."

Well, Teo, if you don't like our methods, you can do your own thing.

But there was something else bothering him.

"Tell me the truth," I asked Teo in Spanish. "What's up?"

"We're wasting crucial time trying to get Cai's dad out."

"What? No. We need to make things right. Tunde's entire village was under the gun. Cai's father is in detention and might never step foot out of prison again. And Ma and Papa aren't getting home without our help. We're the only ones who can fix it. There's nothing more important right now."

Teo stopped walking. "What about Kiran? Seems pretty important to me."

"We're going to stop him."

"If we don't . . . ?"

The others continued ahead before Tunde noticed we weren't following. "Everything's okay," I told Tunde. "Just give me and Teo another minute."

Tunde nodded. "Okay, *omo*. But just a minute."

I turned back to Teo.

"We're going to stop him. We will. We have to."

Teo and I locked eyes for a moment. I wanted him to know how serious I was. How he needed to let go of his stranglehold on the decision making.

"Fine," Teo said. "For now."

2.1

An hour later, we were all squished into a booth at the dumpling place.

It was a small shop with flashing neon lights in the window and greasy tabletops. But the smell! It was an aromatic heaven

inside that restaurant. We'd been in China for several hours, but I hadn't gotten the sense that I was truly in another country until we'd stepped into the dumpling place.

Every scent rang out clear as a bell, and I could not stop my mouth from watering. As we were all starving, we decided it would not hurt to indulge in several rounds of *xiao long bao*, the steamed soup dumplings. They were insanely delicious.

As the waitstaff cleared our plates, a girl, no older than twelve, dragged a plastic chair over to our booth and sat across from us. She was Chinese, short even for her age, and wore an expression of confusion.

"I thought you had blue hair," she said to Cai.

"Rodger Dodger?" Cai asked in response.

"At your service," the girl replied, her English pronunciation flawless.

Teo groaned audibly.

"She's a little girl," he said, motioning to Rodger Dodger.

I shushed him.

"I'm going to tell her what we're up against," Cai told me.

Then, in Mandarin, she gave Rodger Dodger a rundown of our situation. I didn't know much about Rodger, but I assumed Cai trusted her. Only thing she'd mentioned was that they shared a common goal—exposing corruption and malfeasance, soldiers in the same war.

"Well, I don't think I can clear this person's record," Rodger Dodger said in English to all of us. "I don't have that sort of access. But I do think your plan of getting him transferred is possible. Still, it's going to take a significant amount of time to plan properly."

I glanced over at Cai. She looked downcast.

Stressed about her dad.

That's when I got an idea, something a bit out of the box.

"I think I got it," I said. "We go after Terminal first. Naya stole all that data; if we can find her trail, it'll lead us straight to Terminal. If we find them, we can clear Wolf's associate's name. Everything we'll need is with Naya. I say we get the data and then use it to bring Terminal to its knees while we clear Wolf's associate."

Rodger Dodger thought over the suggestion and then looked to me.

She said, "I think it's our only option."

"Sounds complicated," Tunde said. "I want to get Naya just as much as you all do. But there are just as many moving parts in this plan. We do not know where Naya is, to begin. And there are a lot of worries dealing with Terminal—"

"And a lot of risks," Teo said from the other side of the table.

Cai and Rodger Dodger turned to him.

"Don't forget, we already saw Wolf's, uh, *associate* this morning. You were in the detention center, close enough to touch him. It didn't work. And the only reason we're not in a jail cell right now is because our digital prints are still blacked out. We're still, for all intents and purposes, ghosts. We need to stay that way. The second we're recognized on a video feed or a log-in, then Kiran will vanish. Right now, we have the upper hand—he's scrambling. I think it's not in our best interest to get this person out now. We have to take down Kiran first."

No one said anything.

Teo took the opportunity to continue. "We have everything we need," he said. "We can use my bio-computer drives. It won't take long to access them. Then we'll be able to interrupt Kiran's final moves before—"

"I disagree," Cai interrupted. "I think Rex is right. We need to go for Naya and Terminal. It seems the easiest, most logical route."

Tunde cleared his throat.

"I am sorry, *omo*. But Teo has a point. We should hit at Kiran while his defenses are down, and then we can circle back around for Naya, Terminal, and the associate in the detention center. I worry that if we do not take this opportunity to strike at Kiran, the door will close."

"I disagree," Cai said. We were at an impasse.

"So," Teo said, hands on his hips, "what do we do now?"

We all sat in silence for a moment.

Then Tunde spoke up.

"I think I have a very good idea."

2.2

Tunde's idea was simple.

"We split up," he said. "Rex, you and Wolf and Rodger Dodger can track down Naya, and I will go with Teo to the apartment he has in this city. The two of us can begin our work on finding and stopping Kiran."

"I like this plan," Teo said. "My place isn't far."

Cai nodded, and I shook hands with Tunde and Teo.

"Be in touch," I said. "We'll let you know as soon as we find Naya. We can meet back up after and figure out how we'll make it all work."

I watched my best friend walk out into the rain with my brother.

See you guys soon.

And then I turned back to the table where Cai and Rodger Dodger were accessing their network of spies and contacts to attempt to trace Naya's movement after she'd fled Nigeria. Rodger had a small tablet computer ready for the job.

It wasn't easy.

They motioned for me to join them as they navigated terabytes of footage just to find her arrival from Africa. Luckily, Rodger Dodger had some serious skills—while she wasn't a computer expert, she had Cai's quick deductive reasoning.

After Rodger Dodger got us onto Naya's digital scent, Cai jumped in to predict Naya's next moves.

"Naya's communicative," Cai said. "She'll be looking to meet up with Terminal."

"She needs to bring in the data," I said.

"And quick," Cai replied.

We all hunched over Rodger's tablet, watching as Cai sorted through various social media accounts associated with Terminal. She told us she was looking for clues, little giveaways, maybe coded language, that would reveal Naya's plan.

"There," Cai said, pointing to the monitor. "Bread crumbs."

"What is it?" I asked, leaning in to look.

It was a forum for Terminal supporters. They were talking about a "big data haul" and a "triumphant meet-up." But it was all so vague. At least to me.

"She is in Beijing," Rodger Dodger said, looking over the information.

"How do you know?" I asked.

Rodger Dodger pointed to a reference to the 798 Art District.

Cai said, "There's also Terminal chatter, little hints and clues, about what's happening in China right now. Naya's bringing in the data."

"To who?" I asked.

"That is the question," Cai said.

"We need to know where Naya is right now," I said, growing frustrated. "We need to get to her before she hands anything over to . . . whoever."

"We'll get it," Rodger Dodger said. "Just give us a little more time."

I was beginning to feel some of the same frustration that Teo had. Instead of getting antsy, I decided it couldn't hurt to order another round of dumplings. The menus on the wall were, of course, in Chinese. When our waiter came over, I pointed to a picture of some dumplings that looked interesting; he nodded and left.

"Those are delicious," Rodger Dodger said without looking up.

"What's in them?" I asked.

"Mutton," she said.

"Awesome."

Cai elbowed me and whispered, "You're cute."

Then she leaned forward, face inches from the tablet screen, and ran her index finger across a posting on one of the Terminal forums. Rodger Dodger read it and nodded. They high-fived before Cai turned to me.

"Naya's got a customer," Cai said.

"We know who it is?"

Rodger Dodger said, "Looks like Terminal leadership."

"No way," I said, glancing at the screen as if I could read it.

"We do this right," Cai said, "we'll find the head of Terminal."

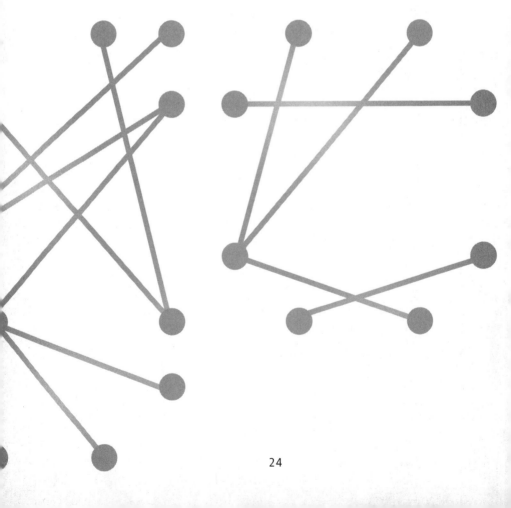

3. TUNDE

Teo and I began the trek to his apartment on foot.

I was happy to be out in the fresh air, despite the rain.

I will tell you that I had an inner peace—a certain stability, a weight from my shoulders—that I had not felt in many, many weeks. With my family and my people safe back in Nigeria, I was now more concerned than ever about ensuring that we accomplished our mission for the sake of my friends. Though I am surely not the bravest of our bunch (that would most definitely be Cai), I did feel the overwhelming urge to ensure we were protected.

Still, I could not shake the unnerving image of the young people that I had seen in the crowds as we made our way to the dumpling shop. They were not tourists. Of that I was certain. And yet they did not appear to belong, either.

I wondered: *Wetin be they palava?*

The streets outside were just as raucous as they had been before. It seemed to me at the time that this was truly a city that never slept.

It did not even take a nap!

As we crossed a busy intersection jam-packed with hundreds of idling vehicles, I felt a bit silly about my worries.

Why was I so nervous? Why was I on edge? No one was looking at me. No one was hiding around a corner. I began to think that my suspicions had been entirely unfounded. Perhaps, I told myself, it was just being in a new city that had me concerned. Though we had traveled so much over the past few weeks, it was likely the strain of our stressful situation had finally gotten the better of me.

Dis stress si mi trouble!

With this thought in mind, I followed Teo across a large plaza that was dotted with trees. People with umbrellas darted to and fro, and I tried to keep up with Teo as he wove expertly through the crowds. That was when I saw them, my friend!

I was not going crazy! I was not overly tired!

There were three young people. They looked very much like contestants at the Game, but these faces were not familiar to me. Two girls and a boy, not much older than the members of the LODGE, stood watching me from across the plaza. They were carefully positioned, the two girls looking at cell phones, while the boy, tall and pale, appeared to be watching the crowds. But I could tell he was actually eyeing me surreptitiously. I knew right away these were the same people who had been following us when we first arrived.

What did they want? Who were they with?

My mind was spinning with questions.

"Tunde?" Teo asked. "What's up?"

He had noticed I had stopped walking and was staring. I turned to tell him what I had seen, but I knew I would have to point out the young people to prove my suspicions. However, when I looked back to where the threesome had been standing, they were gone. Vanished like ghosts back into the rainy night!

"Seriously," Teo said, "are you okay?"

"We are being followed," I told him. "Come."

I started walking with Teo as quickly as I could into the thick of the crowd.

"I thought I was imagining them," I said. "Just being paranoid or something. But it is true, there are three young people following us tonight."

"You recognize them?"

"No. They are new to me."

Teo looked around, eyes tracking every young face in the crowd. "What do these people look like?"

"Young. Not Chinese. Two girls and a boy."

"Think they're with Kiran?" Teo asked.

"I have no idea, but we have to lose them."

Teo and I dodged passersby, darting through the crowd to the edge of the plaza. I noticed an entrance to the subway half a block distant and pointed it out to Teo. "I bet we can lose them in there," I said.

Teo agreed.

As we picked up our pace, racing across another street choked with cars, I pulled out my cell phone and called Cai. She picked up on the first ring. Before Cai could speak, I blurted out my concerns. "Cai," I said, "we are being followed."

"Followed?"

"Yes," I said. "The young people I noticed before we met with Rodger Dodger. I believed then that I was likely mistaken, just being paranoid, but I saw them again just now. We have to meet up. Teo and I will try to lose them here and then—"

"Then run back this way," Cai said.

"I do not think I remember where we were exactly," I said.

I was quite concerned we would easily get lost.

"We'll find you," Cai assured me. "Just move."

3.1

Teo and I raced down the stairs into the subway station.

We tried as best we could to not bump into anyone, but it was difficult.

"The place was, like all of Beijing, ridiculously crowded. At any other moment, I might have complained about the sensation of being packed into this concrete space like sardines in their cans, but at that moment the crowds were a boon.

We reached the first level of the station, where people bought tickets for the train, but realized we did not want to actually jump on a train. We just wanted to give our pursuers the idea that we had.

"There," Teo said, pointing to another staircase that led farther down.

The sound of my shoes on the steps clanged like thunder.

I was running so quickly that I was concerned I would trip and tumble down the stairs. But I realized that if this were the case, I would not mind—I would certainly get to the bottom that much sooner!

At the bottom of the stairs, Teo threw open a door and barreled inside. I reached the door and stopped to look. I could not help myself. Behind us, the staircase was empty. *Perhaps*, I thought, *our plan had worked.*

We found ourselves in a long corridor.

A few people were walking down it toward us, and I realized this was a passageway that ran under the street, likely connecting this station to another a block or so away. It was the perfect deception. We would be like those burrowing rodents I had seen videos of online. When a predator appeared near their homes, they would dart underground and pop up in another location. How clever!

As we sped down the corridor, Teo asked, "Where else did you see these people? You told Cai you'd seen them before."

"Before meeting Rodger Dodger," I said.

"So maybe there's a connection there," he replied.

"No. I doubt that very much," I said. "I know that you are highly suspicious of Rodger, but these people are not associated with her. I do not know how I can confirm that for you, Teo, but I know it is true. Painted Wolf is the most thorough person I know; she would not be fooled by subterfuge."

Though I tried not to act too obviously concerned, I kept turning to look over my shoulder. There were a few people following behind us, but they were not the young people I had noticed in the square. They were just regular folks heading home from work or crossing town for a bite to eat.

"I think we are good," I told Teo.

Teo said, "Just keep moving."

On the other side of the passageway, we found another staircase.

Rather than exiting through the regular entrance to that subway station, we decided to find a side exit. Thankfully, there was a door just to the right of us that was ajar. I pulled Teo by the sleeve and directed him toward the door. He did

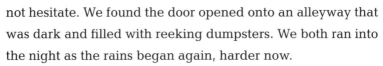

not hesitate. We found the door opened onto an alleyway that was dark and filled with reeking dumpsters. We both ran into the night as the rains began again, harder now.

I did not see the young people who had been tailing us.

It looked as though we were free and clear.

"So where are we going?" Teo asked me.

"Back the way we came," I said.

"That might not be the best idea," Teo replied.

"It is not my idea," I said. "Wolf suggested it."

Teo groaned.

"Sorry, *omo*," I said, "but the Wolf only comes up with good ideas."

3.2

Of course, Cai was true to her word.

Teo and I headed in the general direction we assumed we had run, keeping to the back streets, the darker corners, to avoid CCTV cameras that appeared to be mounted on every light and telephone pole. There were undoubtedly cameras on the rooftops as well. Teo had told us that China was the most surveilled country on the globe, and seeing all those cameras—even though I likely only saw a small percentage of the electronic eyes zooming in on us—certainly made that statement seem all the more certain.

When we stopped at an intersection, my cell buzzed in my pocket.

It was Cai. I answered her call and she said, "To your left."

I looked to my left to see her and Rex standing across the street from us. As soon as the light changed color and the walk sign flashed, Teo and I made our way over to them. I hugged Cai and shook hands with Rex. I could not help it.

Rodger Dodger, however, was not there.

"Where is Rodger?" I asked.

"Lying low," Cai said. "The fact that we're being followed means that someone—Kiran, maybe someone else—is onto us. She can't take any more risks tonight, but she'll be helping online."

Cai motioned for us to follow her.

"Where are we going?" I asked.

My clothes were soaked. There was water in my shoes.

"There," she said.

Cai pointed across the street at a trolley bus that had stopped momentarily to pick up several passengers who were huddled together against the rain.

Beijing trolley bus

"Yes," I said, a bit irritated that I was not getting an actual answer on our destination, "but where does this trolley lead to?"

Cai put a hand on my shoulder. "To Terminal, hopefully."

We ran across the street and made it on board the trolley bus seconds before it pulled out into the street. Cai had a card to pay for our ride (I did notice that the name on the card was not her own), and then we settled into seats in the back. As I sat down, water pooled in the chair and ran down to the floor of the bus. I felt as though I had just swum across the Pacific Ocean.

"We need to get to my place here in Beijing," Teo said. "Now that we have the stuff we'll need to read the data files on a bio-computer, we can—"

"It won't work, Teo," Cai said. She motioned for us all to gather in closely. The bus was not crowded and it did not seem that many of the passengers were paying more than cursory attention to us, but she was wary.

"I thought we already discussed this," Teo said, angry at being interrupted.

"We did, but things have changed. We're being followed now."

"Think they're with Kiran or Terminal?" Rex asked.

"I don't know," Cai said. "Neither would be good."

"Going after Terminal isn't going to help us get Kiran," Teo said as he leaned back in his seat and crossed his arms.

He appeared very unwilling to discuss this situation further.
Dis man wan raina me!

"That's exactly wrong," Cai said. "Terminal will lead us to Kiran. And bringing them down will also clear my father's name. We all thought we'd have time to perfect our plans, but our time has been erased. We cannot plan further; we have to think on our feet. We find Terminal, then we find Kiran."

"What makes you so certain?" Teo asked.

Cai held up one of the cell phones she had acquired from Rodger Dodger.

On the screen was a message posted to a Terminal discussion board. The details were a bit cryptic, as it was written in a coded language and Mandarin. But I immediately noticed the words *OndScan* and *Biswas*.

"It is a post from someone working with Naya," Cai said, translating. "Likely someone who is either a Terminal sympathizer or a Terminal member here in China. The message says they have encrypted information that will compromise Kiran—stolen data that's integral to some secretive OndScan tech. This person claims that if the data can be decrypted, it could take Kiran down."

Rex whistled hearing that. "Wow."

"Wow, indeed," Cai said. "And guess who's going to offer to help?"

6 DAYS UNTIL SHIVA

I knew we were taking a huge risk.

But with Rodger Dodger on the run (and hopefully not caught) and someone on our tail, we simply didn't have any options. I knew Teo was angry. It wasn't an ideal situation to me, either. He wanted to focus on Kiran. But in my mind, this was a way to make everyone happy and, as we say in China, "shoot two birds with a single arrow."

As the bus bumped past Zhongshan Park, I explained the plan.

"We are going to post in this forum answering this person's request. We're also going to ask for an address to meet. I'll do it mimicking the kind of coded language that the poster used. At the same time, I'm going to tip our hand."

"How do you mean?" Tunde asked, suddenly very concerned.

"I'm going to give them hints as to who we are. I think Naya will be even more intrigued if she thinks that we're here after the data she stole. If we offer our assistance, she might see an opportunity."

"An opportunity to screw us over again," Rex said.

"Exactly," I replied.

Tunde looked at me quizzically.

"We want Naya and Terminal to think they can get one over on us. That they have something we desperately need. Something we're willing to make an agreement over. The truth is, of course, that they'll need us more than we'll need them. It'll give us an in, and once we have the data, we can clear my father's name and uncover the rest of Kiran's plans."

Rex looked to his brother. Teo said nothing but shrugged.

"Tunde?" Rex asked.

"I have always said that I trust Cai and her wisdom in these sorts of matters. While I have agreed with Teo that we cannot take risks that might tip Kiran off or lead to our covers being blown, I think we have already crossed that bridge. The people following us are aware we are here. Let us toss the bait to Terminal."

It took me two minutes to compose the message. I was very careful in my wording. The key to making the post convincing was using the right language. I wanted to appear in the know but not **desperate.** I also wanted to make sure that if Naya read the post, she would see the LODGE's fingerprints right away. Tunde was right to call it bait, and once Naya had taken it, the hook would find its mark.

As we waited for the response, I tried to catch my breath. My homecoming had been a nonstop roller coaster ride, and I was eager to take a few moments to orient myself. Looking out the bus windows, I watched the lights of my city drift past. The raindrops on the glass turned each light into a flower of luminance.

While Tunde and Teo talked about the bio-computer, sharing insights on how to wire the machinery, Rex reached

over and took my hand. His grip was so warm. I hadn't realized
how cold my hands were.

Bio-computer

"How are you holding up?" Rex asked.

"I'm okay," I said.

That was only partially true. I was feeling confident that
we could navigate our way through this—we could find Naya,
Terminal, and maybe even get my father out—but I had
my doubts about Kiran. There were just so many factors in
play. While being digital ghosts allowed us to move unseen
(at least until a few minutes earlier), it also kept us in the

dark in regards to Kiran's latest moves. Knowing that there were people after us made me even more concerned about my father. If the authorities could connect us with him (still doubtful but possible), then the likelihood of clearing his name grew ever dimmer.

Seeing my father in shackles was heartbreaking. I couldn't imagine visiting him in an actual prison and seeing him behind bars. It would shatter my mother. And the thought of that almost had me crying. **I had to be strong.** I couldn't give up hope or give in to dark thoughts.

We were still in motion; we just had to stick to the plan.

I asked Rex how he was doing. "Must feel good to have Teo back."

"Yes," he said, glancing over at his brother. "I'd forgotten how cantankerous he can be, but, yeah, it feels . . . I don't know, it feels like we're **even more unstoppable** now. That sounds silly, considering our present situation."

"No, I get it. I like to see that optimism in you. Nice change of pace."

A block from the trolley bus's last stop, we got a response to the posted message. I read it over quickly.

"Did it work?" Tunde was understandably impatient to know.

"Yes," I said. "We have a meeting."

"Excellent," Rex said as he and Tunde high-fived.

"And Naya suspects it is us?" Tunde asked.

"I think so," I said. "But she's playing her cards close to the vest."

"So where are we going?" Teo asked.

"To the opera," I said with a smile.

4.1

Chinese opera isn't like Western opera.

Sure, there are some similarities. Opera is about song and entertainment. But Western opera focuses largely on the voice, whereas Peking opera expands to include dance, mime, and acrobatics. Not to mention the use of string instruments, face painting, and costumes. There is a circus-like element, but it does not have the same sort of childish connotations that circuses have.

For the Chinese, the opera is a matter of cultural pride.

It took two hours and two different buses before we arrived at the opera house Naya had specified in her response to my message. It was at a theater I had been to several times with my parents. There was no show playing at the moment, and the woman at the front desk seemed a bit perturbed to find us knocking on the front door. Finally, after a bit of grumbling, she got up from behind her desk and opened the door a crack.

"We're closed," she said, looking us over.

"I'm sorry," I said. "We were given this address for a meeting."

"Are you performers?" the woman asked.

I nodded, unsure if we'd be convincing.

The woman screwed up her face and pointed to the right. "You need to go into the employee entrance," she said. "Around the corner. Someone should have told you that."

"I agree," I said. "I'm sorry to disturb you."

There was a second entrance, marked EMPLOYEE, on the north side of the building near the delivery ramp. The door was open, and we walked inside to find ourselves backstage and surrounded by amazing costumes. A feathery, gilded dragon, easily twenty feet long with teeth the size of humans, hung above us on a series of ropes and pulleys, and a painted backdrop of a gorgeous sunset loomed overhead. It was like walking into another world.

Opera backstage

"This place is magnificent," Tunde said, looking around. "Next time we have a meeting, we should definitely have it in a place like this."

"You've made it."

The voice came from behind a curtain. We all turned to see a young man with dyed blue hair step into the half-light. He was Chinese and had his hands clasped behind his back. "My name is Cosmo. Follow me."

Cosmo turned and ushered us down a hallway behind the stage.

I'd heard of him before. He was part of the microbloggers' community but didn't post regularly. Most of his stuff had a political edge to it, but I would never have imagined he'd be a Terminal supporter. As we followed Cosmo up a series of stairs, I wondered if he was the person who had been looking for assistance in **decrypting the data** Naya had brought back.

Cosmo led us to a room at the end of a hallway lined by doors that read PERFORMERS ONLY. Two men were standing outside the door. They were Chinese and older than Cosmo. Neither looked like the Terminal type; both more closely resembled hired thugs. The kind of men who wouldn't have a problem kicking you to the floor if someone asked them to.

Cosmo knocked on the door three times.

Then he opened it. The guards stood to the side as we passed through the door into a dressing room lined with mirrors and makeup lights. The door closed behind us. The room was empty outside of a few tables and some hastily arranged chairs positioned in the middle of the room.

"Good to see you, LODGE," Naya said.

She was seated across from us among a collection of familiar faces. Two of them were people I recognized from the Game but whose names I didn't know: prodigies, competitors, but likely people who didn't make it past the first or second round. Sitting right next to Naya was a teenaged girl with long, braided hair. She had dark skin and deep black eyes and wore a kimono. The girl motioned for us to take a seat, and we did. Rex kept his eyes on Naya.

Teo stood at the back of the room near the door.

"My name is Dural Kalali," the teenaged girl with braids said. She spoke with a singsongy Australian accent, and I assumed she was Aboriginal. "Hello, Tunde. Excellent to see you."

Tunde leaned forward in his seat, stunned.

"Dural," he said, flabbergasted. "What are you doing here?"

"This is **my show**," Dural replied. "I am the head of Terminal."

Tunde turned to me and Rex. "She is one of the brightest roboticists in the world. She was not at the Game, but she is known to everyone. Well, at least in the engineering and robotics community. This is quite a shock."

Dural smiled.

"You all are in some big trouble," she said. "And I'm the only one who can help you get out of it."

4.2

"This won't be a bargaining session," Dural continued.

She turned to Naya and nodded.

Naya got up and grabbed a briefcase from a chair in the corner of the room. She brought it over to me and then went and sat back down. I was feeling uneasy already. Dural's confidence was intimidating; I tried to refocus, realizing that our plans were changing by the second, but I needed to get a better read on Dural.

The briefcase was locked.

"The data that Naya brought back from Nigeria—"

"Stole," Tunde interrupted.

"Well," Dural continued, "the data that we now have is not what we anticipated it would be. Sure, it provides insights into Kiran's operations. It has account numbers, passwords, a whole smorgasbord of delicious information. But it also has a puzzling aspect. A key to a lock that we can't open."

"Okay," I said. "What lock?"

"As you're probably aware, Kiran wants to release a program that would cause worldwide devastation. Sink monetary accounts, impact businesses, interrupt governments. Essentially throw the world into chaos."

"Shiva," Rex said.

"Yes," Dural continued, "that is what he calls it. He aims to do this and then release Rama, his fix of sorts—a fix that he can control. While Kiran sees it as a way to rebalance power in the world, to give more to the dispossessed, we see it as a direct threat to our goal of destabilization."

"That's not much of a goal," Rex snickered.

"Well, that can be argued. In our minds, as Terminal, we believe that no one person should have power. So while we can understand Kiran's larger mission, we cannot abide by his methods or support the end result. We have to stop him."

I nodded. "We're agreed on one thing, then."

We'd come here looking to undermine Terminal, but instead it looked like we were going to have to strike a bargain. That was infuriating. Especially since my father's freedom was hanging in the balance.

"To prevent Shiva's release," Dural said, "we need to access a data storage site here in Beijing. It is an OndScan black box lab. Much like the one you visited in India, Rex. While we have what is contained in the briefcase I handed you, Painted Wolf, we don't have a way to successfully breach the systems at the lab."

"So you need help?" Tunde asked.

"Embarrassingly, yes," Dural said.

"You want us to hack into this black box lab?" Rex asked.

Dural shook her head and leaned forward. "No, we could do that. You might assume you're the best coder in this room, but I assure you that you're not. Terminal is, if anything, expert at getting into machines and manipulating software. No, for this mission we need to outsource. We need Tunde and Painted Wolf."

Tunde seemed taken aback. "And why is this?"

"The Beijing black box lab is completely analog. There are no digital systems in the place. No computers, no connections, not even a phone line. All of the data stored inside is bound in books or held on recording tape. Inside the briefcase is a key to get into the building. It is, literally, a key, 3-D printed from **a code hidden inside** the data that Naya smuggled out of Nigeria. We need you to get inside the Beijing black box lab, discover the files that Kiran is hiding there about Shiva, and then bring them back to us in a format we can use."

The room fell silent for a moment as we considered what she was saying.

Terminal was trying to flip the tables on us. Dural was good. Laser focused. That was likely how she'd been able to make Terminal the bane of authorities the world over; she ran a very tight operation. It was going to be difficult to shake her confidence. I realized then and there that I'd have to switch up strategies; we'd need to make her think she was getting exactly what we wanted. Dural was likely used to being challenged, just like she was used to making the decisions. We needed to play on that, to show her we'd be willing to bargain and leave her in charge. I knew she'd never really let her guard down, but if we kept her feeling confident, we might be able to make a move she wasn't expecting.

"And if we do this?" Tunde finally asked.

Dural sat back and folded her hands and said, "Then we will ensure that the individual you were attempting to get out of the Municipal Number 23 detention center is released and all of the charges against him are dropped. That and the fact that you'll be working toward your own goal of stopping Kiran's larger plans."

"And if we decline?" Teo asked from behind me.

Dural shrugged. "Then you'll be **handed over** to the authorities."

"We'll need a while to think it over," I said.

"Fine," Dural said. "There's a room upstairs. You can have the rest of the night. I'll have Cosmo bring you some food and tea."

6 DAYS UNTIL SHIVA

Cosmo took us up to a small room cluttered with junk.

Well, really it was props and costumes, but piled up in the corners of an ill-lit room it pretty much looked like a bunch of junk. There was a folding table that had been set up. On the table were a couple of plates of noodles and a teapot and cups. The noodles smelled good, and I realized it'd been way too long since I'd eaten.

As soon as the door closed behind Cosmo, we started talking.

Tunde spoke first. "This is a joke. We cannot take them up on it."

Cai sat at the table and poured herself a cup of tea.

I sat across from her.

Despite lack of sleep and chaos, she still looked amazing.

Always with the racing heart, huh, Rex?

As she poured she said, "I think it sounds like a reasonable plan. If we can get to the Shiva information, it helps us significantly. And we can free my father."

"That's *if* Terminal holds up their end of the deal," I said.

Cai handed me a cup of tea. It was hot and sweet.

"Let's have a vote. I'm in favor of it," she said.

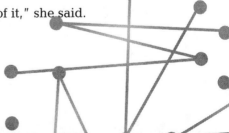

Tunde stood by the door, and I could almost see the wheels turning in his head.

"I do not like it," he said. "This is a very slippery slope we are going down. If we help Terminal, we know that they will try to trick us. Also, it is a matter of morals. We can get this information without their assistance. Better to do it alone, without their help. We have run from the police many times. I am certain that we can run from them successfully again."

Teo, pacing the room, said, "I don't like this. I'm not going to vote."

Tunde just shook his head, disappointed, before turning to me.

"What do you think, Rex? I am against it. Cai is for it."

I took another sip of tea and locked eyes with Cai.

She wasn't the risk taker I was. All of the moves she made, even if they came out of left field, were carefully thought through. If I didn't see the logic behind her decisions, then it was because I wasn't looking closely enough.

If the smartest person in the room agreed to this, I figured I should as well.

"I think we should take the deal," I said. "Sorry, Tunde. I don't think we have any options at this point. And, besides, if we do it right we'll get what we want, too."

"And if it goes wrong?" Tunde asked.

"We won't let it," Cai said. "Now come sit down and eat."

With that settled, Tunde and Teo took seats at the small folding table and helped themselves to paper plates of the noodles and several cups of tea. We ate in silence for a few minutes and then, once full, got down to business.

"So we know off the bat that this thing isn't going to involve much of my skill set," I said. "Tunde and Cai, you're

morals

logic

46

the ones this thing was designed for. My guess is, depending on what exactly this key does, we'll need some mechanical engineering to get through whatever locks there are and social engineering to get past whoever might be in this black box lab."

"But you're the only one of us who's actually been inside one," Cai said.

"I guess that's true," I said. "But I can't imagine this one, being all analog, is anything like the one in Kolkata. However, it probably has some similar people."

"Brain trust people?" Tunde asked.

"Yeah," I said. "You know what they're like."

"We'll still need your skills," Cai said. "Just 'cause it won't be on a computer screen doesn't mean it won't be coding. My guess is that whatever data they've stored there, it's still going to be encrypted. We'll need your math skills."

"Okay," Tunde said. "So we get this information, then what?"

"Then we need to trick Terminal," Cai said. "We can't have them accessing whatever data we pull out of this lab. Even if they want to see Shiva shut down as much as we do, they'll only end up using it for their own goals."

"Maybe those goals aren't as bad as you assume?" Teo said.

I looked over at my brother and noticed he looked quite downcast.

"What does that mean?" Cai asked.

"I'm just saying that maybe Terminal knows something we don't."

"Like what?" Tunde asked.

Teo pushed away his plate of noodles and stood up. He

began pacing the room. Something was wrong with him; he was too stressed, too on edge.

"What's bothering you, brother?" I asked.

Teo stopped pacing and cracked his neck.

He said, "I think it's a bit foolish to waste time on Terminal. This is just the same as wasting time trying to get Wolf's dad out of that detention center. Kiran is the focus here. Kiran is the larger issue! If we don't stop him, no one will. I think you're all being too simplistic and emotional. No one's thinking logically!"

Cai turned to me, concerned.

I stood up and walked over to Teo.

"What're you trying to tell us?"

Teo's face was a snarl of stress. His eyes burned with an anger and confusion I hadn't seen in forever. It was like he was hiding a terrible secret. Something he needed to get out; otherwise he'd burst into flames.

"Please, Teo," I said in Spanish. "It's okay."

Teo sighed long and hard.

Brace yourself, Rex.

"I'm with Terminal," he said.

5.1

I'm not going to lie; I almost punched my brother again.

I balled my fists and started to slug him but held off. It wasn't that the anger subsided—if anything, it just kept growing—but the look in his eyes gave me pause. He looked guilty. He looked disappointed in himself.

"Why?" I asked him, trembling with rage.

"They're doing what most of us don't have the guts to do."

"Destroy everything?"

"Sometimes it's better to wipe the slate clean and start over. Things are terrible out there, Rex. You've been to Africa, to India. You've seen the imbalance. How many people are suffering every second? We live in these perfect illusions, safe behind the mask of thinking we're virtuous people. But right under our noses, poor people are getting poorer. Sick people are getting sicker. The environment is being trashed, the air poisoned. The system is so broken there's no way to fix it now. If we don't so something, something radical, it will only get worse."

"But Terminal isn't about morality, Teo," I said.

He agreed. "I know. But sometimes the end justifies the means."

"People in my country have talked that way," Cai said. "People that I expose for corruption. You might think that fighting fire with fire is the best way to solve this. But that only ends up with everyone getting burned."

Teo turned to me. "Papa always says there's no right way to crack an egg."

"We're talking about civilization, Teo. Not omelets."

"I just think it's silly to automatically assume Terminal's plan wouldn't have worked, that it would have ended poorly—"

"And I think you're wrong to assume otherwise," I said.

Teo replied, "It felt good to belong to something bigger than me. I was helpless at school, learning about history that just repeated itself over and over, the same types of people making the same types of mistakes. Terminal offered to do something about it. That's all I really wanted. The world's going one way; Kiran's going another. Terminal offered the only alternative, and now . . ."

He slouched against the wall.

"I'm not going to pretend that they have everything figured out. Or that they haven't made mistakes," Teo continued. "But I do think that they can get this thing done, they can take down Kiran and send a message to the world in the process. I don't think this will be the end but the start of something bigger."

I couldn't believe what I was hearing. This whole time, ever since that night in the garden in Kolkata, I'd sincerely believed that my brother hadn't abandoned my family—our family—to join a hacktivist cell bent on mayhem.

Even when the clues were there, I denied them.

Even when my friends had suggested it might be true, I ignored them.

And yet Teo, my own flesh and blood, had deceived me.

I couldn't put into words how crushed I was.

But hit by a speeding bus might be close.

"Does Dural know who you are?" Cai asked.

"No," he said. "They don't know my name or my face. They only know my handle online. I've been helping them for the past fourteen months, but it's been at a distance. Dural has never interacted with me."

"But you would protect them?" Tunde wanted to clarify.

Teo didn't answer.

"Don't put me in a position of not trusting you, brother," I said, wanting to punch Teo again. "Answer the question. If we do this job, get that information on Shiva, and then hand it over to Terminal, are you going to warn them that we will be trying to double-cross them?"

"I'm just letting you know what I think. I don't agree with

everything Terminal does. Heaven knows I've had my battles with them—"

Teo shook his head.

Tunde stood up.

"This is silly," he said. "I am not going to work with Terminal, and I am certainly not going to trust your brother. I am sorry, Rex. This pains me very deeply, but I must not be a part of this."

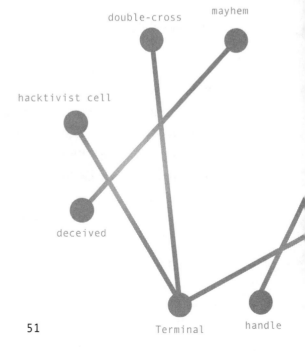

double-cross   mayhem

hacktivist cell

deceived

    Terminal   handle

6. TUNDE

6 DAYS UNTIL SHIVA

My friends, I stood up then and there.

I could not see how this would work in a way that would benefit us. I had witnessed firsthand how much damage someone like General Iyabo could do. I could only imagine that if we got Terminal the information for Shiva, they could unleash havoc across the globe.

The realization that Teo would be in league with such people was disheartening to say the least. To think of the weight that it placed upon the shoulders of my best friend was truly upsetting. I worried it would do psychological harm to Rex.

"I am telling you," I said aloud to Cai and Rex, "that I know deep down in my soul, in the very depths of my being, that nothing good can come of this arrangement. It is better for us to take our chances with the authorities than do the bidding of this organization. When this idea was first suggested, by you, Cai, it was to trick Terminal, not to help them!"

"We will be tricking them," Rex said.

"I cannot be sure it will work," I replied. "It is simply too risky."

Rex turned to Cai. She had not spoken in a few minutes

and appeared to be contemplating her next move. Sadly, she had the most to lose in this arrangement. While we were going to attempt to stop both Terminal and Kiran, it was the life of her own father that hung most precariously in the balance.

"Before I make a decision," Cai said, "I need more information from Teo."

"Fair enough," Rex said, looking to Teo.

Teo crossed his arms, ready to answer. Though, judging by his expression and the fact that he did not seem very apologetic earlier, I doubted she would like what she heard.

"When we arrived in China," Cai began, "was your intention always to bring us to Terminal? Was there a bigger scheme in the works?"

"No," Teo said. "I'm here to help you stop Kiran. That's never changed."

"And you weren't going to involve Terminal?"

"Not unless I needed to."

"I do not like that answer," I said. "There should never be a time or an instance when you would need to involve such people."

Rex raised his hand, asked me to be quiet for a moment.

Then Rex asked Cai: "What do you think?"

Cai slumped back in her seat and said, "I'm sorry, Tunde. But I really don't think we have much of a choice. My father is caught up in this. I need to get him out of that detention center before he's shipped off to a prison and never seen again. I can't guarantee that we'll pull this off, that we can get the information to stop Kiran, clear my father, and at the same time pull the rug out from under Terminal. But I think we need to try."

It seemed that I was outvoted. And yet, I have to tell you,

my friends, that I could not go through with it. My mother did not raise someone who is fast and loose with his morals. This was one thing I had to stand against.

At the same time, I could not just let my friends, my dear and best friends, wander off into the mouth of danger with no assistance. I thought back to our time in my village. How Cai had so craftily and carefully manipulated the men who worked under General Iyabo. How she had created illusions and used her social engineering skills to manipulate situations.

Surely, I could do such a thing?

I learned so much from watching her that I surely could find a way to ensure my friends were safe and at the same time had an outside hand in this operation. Even if I was capable of doing only a tenth of the magic Cai did, it would be a tremendous boon to our success.

My friends, I am not ashamed to tell you that I did just that. And to make it as believable as possible, I raised my voice and even held up my fist to show my, admittedly exaggerated, anger.

"Fine!" I shouted. "If that is your decision, then you can count me out."

With that, I stormed out of the room, making sure to knock my shoulder into Teo as I passed him. Before I slammed the door, I looked back at Rex and Cai and saw the surprise and shock on their faces.

My scheme had worked.

6.1

My friends, I had to be deceptive to protect Rex and Cai!

As I left the room and ran down the stairs to the lower level of the opera house, my heart was thundering in my chest with worry.

I did not hear them chasing after me but moved as quickly as I could regardless. If Rex had caught up with me and tried to convince me to come back, I feel as though my resolve might have crumbled.

For my plan to work, I needed to get away quickly.

Though I was deeply upset at seeing Rex so heartbroken and betrayed, I knew that working with Terminal, especially considering that Teo was part of their organization, was going to be very tricky. We would need some outside help. And there was no one that needed help more than me.

I realized as I barreled through the employee entrance out into the night that I was putting them in a difficult situation. Dural said that she needed my expertise to unlock the information at the Beijing black box lab, but I also knew that Rex and Cai would be able to pull this off without me. Especially since I would, of course, still be helping—just not in sight of Teo and Terminal.

Luckily for me, the rain had stopped and traffic had slowed. I went to the nearest intersection and grabbed my cell phone from my pocket. Now I just had to pray that the next step would work.

I called Rodger Dodger.

I was not sure she would answer a random call, but then again, Cai had said she had agreed to help and had given us this number. The phone rang three times, but just before I hung up and considered my other options, she answered.

"Tunde?" she said.

"Yes," I replied. "How did you know it was me?"

"I'm good at what I do. Is everything okay?"

I said, "I need to meet with you. Are you available?"

Rodger Dodger took a moment, then replied, "Things have gotten pretty hot around town. Painted Wolf told me you're being followed. I've already taken a lot of risks meeting you guys earlier. Not sure I can do it again."

"It would just be with me," I said. "I apologize for pulling you into this, probably deeper than you anticipated going, but we are on the cusp of something quite significant and I need your help very badly. This is momentous."

"Define momentous."

"Well," I said, "it involves Terminal. . . ."

Rodger Dodger was silent for a second. "Are you kidding?"

"No," I said. "Will you help me?"

"I can be at your location in about twenty-five minutes. Stay right where you are. Is everyone else okay? They are not with you?"

"Yes and no," I said. "I have a lot to explain."

True to her word, Rodger Dodger showed up in a taxicab exactly twenty-seven minutes later. As I waited, I watched the crowds, looking for the young people who had been following us. Thinking back, I realized the last time I had taken a moment to really observe my surroundings in such detail was on my way to the Game so many days back! My friends, it felt like ancient history.

I climbed into the backseat of the cab beside Rodger Dodger, and she told the driver a few words in Mandarin. This gentleman had quite the lead foot, and the car immediately sped off into traffic at a ridiculous rate of speed. My stomach nearly leaped out of my mouth!

"Tell me what is going on," Rodger Dodger said in English.

I glanced up at the taxicab driver.

"He only speaks Mandarin," she said. "Don't worry."

I told Rodger Dodger of the plan with Terminal and my deception. She understood my plan and agreed that I had done the right thing. While it would not have been so much as a moral quandary for her, she thought it was quite wise of me to provide that "outside man" angle. It would be, in her words, crucial.

As the cab ascended a ramp onto an elevated highway, Rodger Dodger handed me an encrypted and untraceable cell phone. She told me that she kept many such phones and that while they were quite expensive, she saw them as a necessity for her line of work. I understood completely and thanked her profusely.

After logging in to a secure messaging app that the LODGE had used in the past, I composed a message intended for Cai and Rex only.

It was quite simple:

Dear LODGE—I am not truly angry. The fight was a fake. I stormed out of the room merely to convince Teo that I was not going to help. But I am. I will do it from outside. Please contact me as you learn more about what you are going to do. Rodger Dodger and I will help you. Please do not worry. Everything will be okay! You can do this! But be very, very careful. See you soon.

Eleven minutes later, the taxicab pulled up at a massive apartment building.

We exited the car, and as we walked into the foyer, Rodger Dodger explained that this was the place where her aunt lived. The good news was that her aunt traveled frequently—she was a steward for an airline—and that the apartment would be empty for at least another few days.

"The best part," Rodger Dodger said, "is that my aunt has something of a sweet tooth and the apartment is well stocked with ice cream and candy."

I could think of nothing better right then.

Rex and I were shaken by Tunde's sudden departure.

After he'd stormed out of the room, we assumed he would reappear in a matter of minutes. When those minutes passed and he hadn't come back, we started to worry. I was also worried about Rex. He was furious with Teo. Before, it had been about his brother's deception, but now it was also about Tunde's hasty departure.

"He'll be fine," Teo said, as though that might smooth things over.

"You can be a real jerk," Rex told his brother as we made our way downstairs to talk to Dural and tell her we had agreed to carry out the black box lab mission.

Dural was, as expected, happy to hear of our decision.

"Excellent," she said. "The right choice."

Dural produced the briefcase she'd handed me before and proceeded to unlock it. Inside was the 3-D key she told us had been printed; it was a **skeleton key** and it looked quite ordinary, except it wasn't made of metal and there was a clear plastic disk embedded in the top of the key—the disk was about an inch in diameter. Other than the key, there were blueprints of the Beijing black box lab. Dural told us they were exceedingly hard to come by but that they were accurate.

Rex, Teo, and I looked over the drawings. Rex said that the building closely resembled the one he had been inside in India. It had a very similar layout with an equivalent number of rooms. That meant a similar number of staff.

"I'm guessing," Rex said, "that most of the people in here are going to be from Kiran's brain trust. The ones I met in India were real hangers-on. They never doubted a thing that Kiran said or did. No doubt word has spread about my time in India; chances are if they recognize me they're going to sound the alarm."

"Maybe we use disguises," I suggested.

"Well," Rex said, looking around the room, "we are in a theater."

"You won't need them," Dural said as she walked over to us and looked at the **blueprints**. "The black box lab will be empty. While we can't access the material inside the building, we are quite skilled at everything leading to it. We'll arrange for an early morning 'accidental' gas leak in the buildings nearby. The police will shut down the entire neighborhood as a precaution, and they'll empty out the black box lab. So, once you're in, you'll be free to get the data for us."

Rex looked at me, catching the same thing I did.

"Hang on," I said. "When exactly do you expect us to do this?"

Dural grinned. "Tomorrow morning, obviously."

"Doesn't give us much time to plan," I said.

With everything that had happened, I needed the bedrock

of my strategizing time. I wasn't sure that having a single night, barely five hours, would suffice.

"I think you're more than capable," Dural said. "The LODGE thinks fast on its feet, right? We both have something we want. No point in delaying it. You can sleep here, rest up, and then in the morning tackle the black box. If anything, I think you've got something of a luxury of time. You've been running across the globe in a panic—take the rest of the night to recover. By the way, Cosmo told me that Tunde left a little bit ago. Seems he was in a bit of a huff. A real shame, that. You three think you're capable of doing this without him?"

"Do we have much of a choice?" Rex asked.

"Good point," Dural said. "See you in the morning."

As Dural turned to leave, I asked, "What exactly will we be looking for?"

Dural didn't answer.

As she stepped out of the room, Rex, Teo, and I returned to the blueprints. Even though they laid out the interior of the building, the plans gave no hint at how the data was stored inside. Books? Microfiche? **It could be anything.**

So that left us with a few hours to come up with a vague plan and get some much-needed sleep. Being forced into this arrangement with Terminal made me anxious. Not only did we have to pull off our original objectives, but we'd have to double-cross Dural on top of it. Having Tunde storm out only made things that much more unstable. Strategizing the next twenty-four hours was going to take every ounce of skill I'd ever developed.

At that moment, both Rex's and my cell phones buzzed.

It was a message from Tunde.

After reading it, Rex glanced over at me and grinned.

7.1

We strategized as best we could for two hours, then we spent a fretful three trying to sleep on the floor.

Just before dawn, Dural drove us personally to the site.

Her car was, oddly enough, a minivan. Gray and very dull, it seemed the perfect vehicle for someone hiding in plain sight. Rex, Teo, and I climbed into the back of the van with the few tools Dural offered us—our cells, lock picks, screwdrivers, magnifying glasses, and flashlights.

We drove in silence. I knew the sections of the city we were passing through, and it was strange seeing them at that hour under such odd conditions. I thought about my mother. It had been several days since I'd contacted her, and I was certain she was worried. I made a mental note that regardless of what happened at the black box lab, I would call her in the morning.

As the traffic cleared and the van picked up speed, Rex reached over and put his hand on mine. I squeezed his hand and worried that mine was clammy. We'd been under so much stress, I was half-surprised my hands weren't shaking.

"We got this," Rex whispered, leaning in.

"We've spent enough time around Tunde to have picked up a few skills."

"Mostly he just seems to design outrageously over-complicated machines."

I laughed at that, thinking back on the highwall machine.

Then, my thoughts returning to the mission at hand, I said, "I just need to **get my father out** of this mess. Seeing him in that detention center was . . . It was horrible. I want to make sure I never see him like that again."

Rex squeezed my hand.

Five minutes later we arrived at the neighborhood, an industrial block of the city, and were ushered through a roadblock manned by a multitude of police officers after Dural waved an ID badge. As we drove past the cops, Dural looked at us in the rearview mirror and held up the ID.

"We could teach you guys a thing or two."

I declined to acknowledge that.

The Beijing black box lab was a rather plain-looking building. Brick and steel, it was two stories tall and had no windows. It resembled nothing more than a big brick box, and it sat on a corner, squeezed between two glass office buildings.

"The one in India look like this?" Dural asked Rex.

He leaned forward to get a better look.

"No," he said as she stopped the car. "That one was fancier."

Dural hit a button and the back door of the minivan slid open, letting the humid night air waft inside. "When you've got it," she said, "you call me."

Dural handed me a scrap of paper with a phone number on it.

"You never told us what we're looking for," I said.

"You'll know it when you see it."

Rex, Teo, and I got out of the minivan and made our way toward the building. I had the 3-D printed key in my hand. Rex lifted up a strip of police tape so we could duck under it and head toward the black box lab's front door.

"Power's out," Rex said, pointing to dark streetlamps.

"I think we can assume the cameras are down, too," Teo added. He motioned to several camera arrays mounted on the outside of the building.

"I would not assume anything," I said.

I pulled one of the flashlights out and shined the laser pointer at the **camera array**, hitting each of the cameras' light sensors. If they were recording, they weren't now. Rex turned and gave me a wink.

We mounted the stairs, and I pulled the 3-D key from my pocket. I was shocked the lock on the front door wasn't a biometric or a retinal scan lock. It was a good lock, solid, heavy, but still a mechanical one that I could pick. I suppose the whole concept of keeping the Beijing black box lab analog extended to the front door. An electronic lock could surely be hacked—if anything, Kiran was consistent.

The 3-D key didn't work.

"This isn't the right one," I said.

"Must be for something else, then," Teo added.

It took me two minutes and six seconds to pick the lock on the door.

That was a surprisingly long time.

It wasn't nerves and I wasn't getting rusty—the lock had a few tricks up its proverbial sleeve. For starters, it was upside down; a simple but effective deterrent for a less-than-patient picker. Second, the pin tumblers inside were sticky. No doubt that was intended.

Regardless, I got it open.

Before going in, I turned to Teo. "Can you stand guard?"

He scoffed. "Seriously? You want me to wait out here?"

"Given everything that's come out," I said, "I think it's best."

I looked to Rex. He put a hand on his brother's shoulder.

"Teo," he said, "you lied to us. Besides, we need someone on the lookout. I don't trust Dural, and I never would have gotten as far as I have if I believed everything everyone told me. Please, just keep an eye out for us."

Teo mulled it over as though we were giving him a choice.

"Fine," he said. "But you call me if anything comes up that you can't handle."

"Of course," I said.

Rex and I stepped in, flashlights out, to find a narrow hallway that led to a larger room. Inside, the lights were already on.

7.2

The place seemed to be empty, however.

As Dural had told us, the neighborhood and all of the surrounding buildings had been evacuated on the pretense of a gas leak. When the black box lab had been cleared out, it was done so in a hurry. First thing I noticed when we walked in was a cup of coffee sitting on a desk by the front door. There was a half-eaten croissant sitting next to it. Still looked fresh.

"Okay," Rex said, "this is different."

The blueprints were wrong. I doubt that Dural had messed up and gotten the wrong plans. More likely, whoever built this place for Kiran had submitted different blueprints to the government before construction began; either that or they'd been really busy remodeling the place.

There was only one room: one giant, two-story open room that resembled a library. Everything was beige. The carpets, the walls, the furniture, even the lighting fixtures—all a dull, washed-out sand color. And that made it **nearly impossible** to pick out particular objects—it was like a fun house gaff, the kind where someone wears a shirt the same pattern as the wallpaper and "hides" right in front of you.

"So **where do we even begin?**" Rex asked.

Though there were desks, chairs, and some couches along the walls, the central area of the room was filled with row upon row of bookshelves. On the bookshelves were books, all bound in identically colored beige leather covers. Every book, from first glance, appeared to be approximately the same size. Each shelf held at least three or four hundred books. That meant there were thousands in the room.

I pulled the 3-D key back out.

"We start with this."

First thing, we explored the perimeter of the room. We had to make sure there weren't any additional side rooms that we couldn't see, any alcoves or places where they might have hidden something. We couldn't find any. It looked as though the room was the entirety of the building and that meant that the key was intended to unlock something we'd already seen.

"Hang on." Rex put out his arm to block me from taking another step.

We were on the far side of the room from the door, and I didn't see anything in front of me that looked worrying. Just a beige couch, a small desk with nothing on it, and a standing lamp.

"Look," Rex said, crouching down and pointing at the ground.

Three inches above the carpet was a wire. It was metal, not clear fishing line, but it was **nearly invisible**. It stretched across the floor, taut, from the wall to a bookshelf. If there was one, that meant there were likely many others.

"How'd you even see that?" I asked.

Rex said, "Honestly, it was kind of an accident. I thought my shoelace was untied, and when I glanced down to look, I noticed it."

"What do you think it does? Alarm system? Trap?"

"Trap?" Rex laughed. "Like in a mummy's tomb or something?"

"I'm not kidding. I wouldn't put anything past Kiran. He's desperate."

Rex lay down on his stomach in front of the wire and then traced it with his eyes from the bookshelf to the wall. At the wall, it went into a small hole, just the right diameter to contain the wire.

"Whatever it does," he said, "I don't think we should mess with it."

We stepped over the wire and nothing happened. But ten yards away, we found another one. This time I spotted it first. It went across the room in a similar fashion, from one bookshelf to another. But this one wasn't three inches from the ground— it was four feet off the ground, right at chest level.

Black box lab

"This is ridiculous," Rex said. "No one could work in here like this."

"They must have put them up when they were leaving."

"Or no one actually works in here," he suggested.

"Then what?"

"It could be just a storage place."

"What explains the croissant?" I asked.

Rex shrugged. "Maybe there's a guard."

Our cell phones buzzed in our pockets simultaneously. We took out our phones to see a text from Tunde. We hadn't contacted him since Dural had dropped us off, and he was concerned. He asked if we were having any troubles. I replied to him that we were okay. Then I opened a video messaging app and called him. He answered right away, and it was nice to see his smiling face in the midst of all the dull beige.

"Tunde," I said, "check this out."

Using my phone, I panned across the room and then brought the cell camera lens close to the trip wire. I went along it, showing him both ends so he could see how it was tethered. "What do you think?" I asked.

"I do not think it is designed to bring down the bookshelves or to set off an alarm," Tunde said. Then he asked, "Can you show me the ends of it again?"

I did. "Now move the camera up, toward the ceiling."

After he'd gotten a good look at the bland, featureless ceiling tiles, he asked me to examine the bookshelf where it was tethered more closely. I held the camera as close as I could. He noticed that there was a cylindrical object embedded in the wood panel on the bookshelf. It was silver and black and the size of a pinkie finger.

"What is it?" Rex asked.

"A blasting cap, I think," Tunde said.

"Hang on, what?"

"Friends," Tunde said, his voice deep with concern, "I need the two of you to be incredibly careful in this place. That is a **blasting cap**. I have seen similar ones before. They are used to set off charges. My guess, and this is just a guess, is that the room in which you are standing is wired to explode, or maybe only burst into flames, if you set off one of those trip wires."

"*Only* burst into flames?" I asked.

7.3

Rex and I looked around the room.

All the books, all the wooden shelves, the furniture, even the chairs, were made of wood. A single match would likely light this place up like a bonfire. And all of the information contained inside it would be nothing more than smoke in a matter of minutes—including whoever was unfortunate enough to be inside at the time of ignition.

"That's why this place is empty," Rex said. "They're not taking chances."

"Just means that whatever's in here is worth protecting. Let's find it."

We discovered three additional trip wires around the room. There were no other places where the 3-D key might work, so we focused our efforts on the bookshelves. Outside of the five trip wires, there were only thousands of the identical-looking books. Rex and I took several down from the shelves and thumbed through them carefully.

"These are **lines of code**, just printed out," Rex said, turning pages.

He moved from shelf to shelf, quickly glancing through the books. He must have looked at a dozen before he walked over to where I was and glanced over my shoulder at the book I was holding. Every single book contained page after page of computer code. There were many different coding languages—some simple, others incredibly complex—and they covered all sorts of programs.

Rex deciphered them as he read.

"This one is about timing on a fan, that one's for camera movement. They're all kind of just garbage codes, nothing special, not even clever. It's like if you just dumped all the manuals you got with every electronic item you purchased—a toaster, a cell phone—into a library and made them fancy."

He motioned to the rest of the library.

"This is a con," he said. "None of this is useful. None of it worth burning."

"So that means the key is for something else."

Rex's cell phone rumbled. It was a text from Teo.

Might need to hurry it up. There's someone down the street—looks like a police officer or something—he's going door-to-door, checking on the buildings. He's moving pretty slow, but I'm guessing he'll be here in about five minutes. I can try to distract him, but you need to get a move on.

Rex showed me the message. We were going to have to think on our toes. Searching for a keyhole in that black box lab was going to be nearly impossible. It might be hidden under the carpeting or up on the ceiling. But I was certain it wouldn't be random. The data Naya stole that led to the printing of the key was kept secret. If anyone was able to print the key, then that meant it was supposed to be used—finding the key was the trick, not where it went.

I had an idea. The only way we'd uncover the purpose of the 3-D key and the real reason all this junk code was filed away in this bland analog library was intuiting why Kiran would put it here in the first place. The Game, OndScan, the data stolen by Naya, it all came from Kiran—his creation, guided by his hand.

"What if the key isn't a key?" I asked Rex.

"How do you mean?"

"I'm trying to think like Kiran here. A key is so obvious. Someone gives you a key, you're going to start looking for a lock, right?"

"Yeah . . ." Rex looked a bit confused.

"So what if it's not the lock that's important but the key itself?"

I took the 3-D printed key out of my pocket and examined it in the flat light. If the key wasn't designed to open something obvious, then maybe it was to be used in a different way—the answer, of course, was in the clear disk at the top of the key.

It wasn't a disk. It was a lens.

"I think I figured this out," I told Rex as I walked to the center of the room, in the only space clear of bookshelves and trip wires, and held the top of the key to my eye. Sure enough, I had been right—the key wasn't a key.

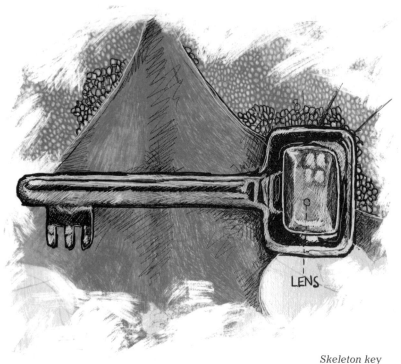

Skeleton key

Looking through the lens I could see the library, the bookshelves, but overlaid on top of what I was seeing was a grid. It was three-dimensional and a neon-blue color. I smiled; this was very, very clever.

"What are you seeing?" Rex asked.

"It is an **augmented-reality overlay**," I said. "There is a grid over the room."

As I turned my head, the lines moved with me. To my surprise, big blue arrows appeared and hovered digitally over the locations where the trip wires were hidden. Looking farther, some of the books on the shelves were lit up in the neon blue as well. I walked over to one—through the lens, the spine and cover were glowing an eerie blue. I could see fifteen other books highlighted the same way.

"There are specific books," I said to Rex as I handed him one. "Whatever code is hidden in this library, it is probably in these."

It took us several minutes to grab all the highlighted books. As we pulled the last one from its shelf, Teo texted to let us know time was running out. And fast. The man inspecting the nearby businesses was crossing the street toward him. We had to go; there was no more time to explore the library.

Still, we couldn't just hand these books over without understanding what they contained. While we could have examined them carefully on the journey back to the opera house, I was worried about having Teo look at them with us. Given that he'd admitted involvement with Terminal, I wanted to take precautions.

Rex and I piled the books on a desk near the front door.

We thumbed carefully through the pages, and Rex read through the code as quickly as he could. "These are just the same junk programs," he said. "There's nothing about these books that makes them any different from the others."

Teo texted again: *Hurry—the man wants to come inside.*

I could feel my blood pressure rising behind my eyes, my heartbeat quickening; we had to at least get a cursory sense of what these things were. We could be handing Terminal the keys to Kiran's empire. **That is when I saw it**—a series of shapes, mostly lines and dots, running along the bottom right corner of each page. They looked like pieces of letters and numbers.

"What about that?"

I pointed out the lines and dots to Rex. He flipped through the book, looking them over. "Yes," he said, eyes glued to the pages, "there's something there."

As Rex turned the pages faster and faster, I figured it out.

"Here," I said, picking up one of the other books. Holding it by the spine, I flipped through the pages as fast as I could. As we watched, the lines and dots, bits and pieces, came together when the pages were in motion. They formed numbers at the bottom of the pages. Suddenly the purpose of the books became clear as the numbers **danced and moved**, appearing to scroll across the page.

"It's a flip-book," I said. "They're all flip-books."

Flip-book

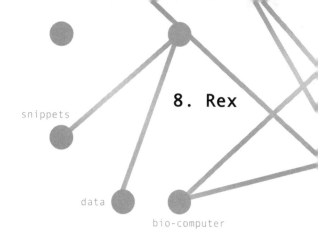

5 DAYS UNTIL SHIVA

Cai was right.

The books, all fifteen of them, were basically a big version of a kid's toy.

You know those flip-books you buy at the zoo or the museum?

The ones that you flip and they show you a dinosaur stomping across some primordial swamp or a rocket ship jetting between the stars?

Well, this was the same way, but instead of some cool illustrated scene, they showed me a long series of program codes, most of which I recognized immediately. I flipped through as many of the books as I could, just enough to get a sense of what they were hiding, before Cai and I stacked them in our arms and headed to the door.

"It's all here," I told Cai. "The snippets of code that I was able to read include pieces of WALKABOUT 2.0, some of the data Naya stole from General Iyabo, and big chunks of Teo's bio-computer stuff."

"What does it do?"

"I'm not sure what Kiran intended," I said, "but this is the kind of thing that would get Terminal's heart really racing. From what I can tell, it's a virus."

"A virus?"

We stopped at the door. I was keenly aware that my brother, a now-known Terminal associate, was standing just on the other side. Even though it wasn't necessary, I still lowered my voice.

"All these disparate elements come together in this code. It's kind of sloppy, clearly written pretty quickly, but it works like this: The data that Naya stole from General Iyabo has the names and address of the target accounts—banks, international companies, conglomerates, even governments. Those accounts are entered into the WALKABOUT 2.0 program, which covertly populates them with back door access programs. Then Teo's bio-computer tech acts as massive organic processors, able to store all the data necessary to distribute the virus to all of the accounts. Essentially, this thing is a stealth bomb."

"To blow up what?"

"All global trade."

It wasn't until the words left my mouth that I realized how big this whole thing was. At the Game, Kiran had used WALKABOUT and the quantum computer to hack into thousands of accounts—stealing data on banking, business, etc. But this was the reverse; this would be putting a virus into those accounts to destroy them.

"If this thing gets out," I told Cai, "it'll do some serious, probably unrepairable damage. It'll wreck countries. Economies will collapse. People will die."

"Shiva," Cai said.

"In Kiran's hands, yes," I replied.

"But in Terminal's hands?"

"Even worse," I said.

We both looked at each other, knowing that we'd just found ourselves in an incredibly delicate situation—we had our hands on an explosive and we had to do something with it. We certainly couldn't let Kiran use this virus for his Shiva program; we also couldn't let Terminal take it over.

Both routes were dead ends.

Literally.

"So what do we do?" I asked Cai.

She flashed me her trademark Painted Wolf smile.

"You'll be shocked to hear this, but . . . I've got a plan. When we get outside, you're going to call Tunde and tell him what we need. Some sort of scanner, to scan the pages of these books and extract the code; then, while it's being translated into a form they can use, we'll alter it."

"Alter it how?"

"That's what you're going to figure out."

8.1

We opened the door and stepped outside to find Teo arguing with a security guard.

At least, the guy looked like a security guard.

He didn't speak English, and Teo was stumbling through some ugly Mandarin. I was never the languages type—that was always one of Teo's fortes—but I knew that his Mandarin was always the weakest of the six languages he'd taught himself.

Cai took right over.

Handing the books to Teo, she spoke to the security guard,

gesticulating wildly with her hands. The conversation got heated for a few moments before the security guard put up his hands and backed away. He moved on, walking over to the next building on his route.

"All good?" I asked Cai.

"We're good," she said.

Truth is: I was curious to know how she'd run the guy off, but, frankly, we didn't have time to discuss it. We needed to know how we were going to hand the flip-books with a dangerous virus in them over to the one group of people who we knew should never have them.

As we walked back toward the road and out of the restricted area, Teo asked about what we'd found inside the building.

"First off," I said, "Dural's blueprints were totally off. It was an analog library, but it was one giant room lined with trip wires and explosives."

"Explosives?" Teo honestly seemed shocked.

"Kiran was pretty serious about protecting the place."

Teo asked, "So what was he protecting?"

"Those books," Cai said.

Teo tsked. "This is like pulling teeth. Just tell me what's up."

"There's a code hidden in those books," I said. "We're not sure what it does, but it'll have to be extracted."

"Hidden how?"

"These fifteen tomes are flip–books; the code can only be seen by flipping the pages fast. Pretty impractical, while clever," I said.

"Any idea what the code does?" Teo asked.

I shrugged. "We're just going to have to find out. Hang on. . . ."

I pretended I was getting a call, and instead of answering a call, I surreptitiously called Tunde. I slowed my pace and then signaled Cai before I turned around and jumped onto the call.

Tunde said, "I am ready, *omo*. Tell me what we need to do."

"We've got fifteen books with codes hidden inside them. Essentially, they're big flip-books that we—"

"Flip-books? What are flip-books?"

"Seriously? It's a book that, uh, you flip. The pages, I mean, you flip the pages and usually there's a picture that becomes animated on them. Sometimes they're photos that move, like how a movie works—"

"Flick books! Yes, I am familiar with these."

"Well, great. That's what we're dealing with here. Kiran, clever bastard that he is, hid a code inside the flip, er, flick books. From what I can tell, just after a brief look, this thing is a virus. A virus designed to bring down economies, to ruin countries."

"Shiva," Tunde said.

"Yes. And we can't let Terminal get ahold of it."

"Ah," Tunde said, getting snarky, "this is exactly the thing that I was warning you two about. I did not want to involve Terminal—"

"Tunde," I interrupted, "too late for that. Listen, we're going to have to hand over these books. But Terminal can't use them unless they write the code down, which is painstaking in the extreme. I need you to build a scanner, something that will photograph the pages, pull the code out, and piece it together. These books are the size of dictionaries. Each one has at least five hundred pages."

"Okay. Okay. But there is a twist, right?"

"There's always a twist, Tunde. We're going to change the code in the scanner. Render it useless. But not in a way that will be obvious. I need Terminal to accept the code and then use it. That's when we spring the trap."

"When the code is activated, it alerts the authorities."

"And brings Terminal down, clears Cai's parents, clears everyone. That's a tall order, I know, but let's see how clever we can make it."

Tunde laughed. I could picture him grinning on the other end of the line.

"Of course, my friend. The machine will be easy to build, provided I can find all the necessary supplies quickly. You are going to have to help me, however, with the code and how we change it. Tell me, how much time do I have?"

"I don't know, I'd guess a couple hours?"

I looked back at Teo and Cai. They were standing on a corner just on the other side of the police tape, and a group of police officers were standing about and smoking. I waved to Teo and he waved back.

"Do you define a couple as two or more than two?" Tunde asked.

"Better make it two."

Just then, a car drove up; it was the same car that had dropped us off.

Dural was behind the wheel.

"Big moment," I told Tunde.

"We are ready. Let us bring them down."

8.2

As we drove back to the opera house, books in hand, I couldn't help but glance over at my brother and feel a knot in my stomach.

I'd only just found him.

After so many years of wondering, so many sleepless nights spent formulating plans of how to find him, designing WALKABOUT, now I was faced with the awful reality—to save Cai's parents, to stop Kiran, I'd have to bring down Terminal and Teo with it.

The thought gave me chills.

What would my parents think? Selling out my brother?

I knew I had to find a way to bring him to our side, to convince him to give up Terminal and make the right decision. The LODGE was family. I had to show him that Terminal's plan meant disaster and that he could change the world with me.

Thing is, I had to do it before the scanner completed its work.

And somehow keep the truth of what we were doing from Dural.

"Did the plans work?" Dural asked, leaning back to look at me.

"No," I said. "They didn't."

"Not at all?"

Cai said, "I think you misjudged your sources, Dural. The building had been completely remodeled. It was nothing like the plans. There were no employees inside and a lot of traps. You sent us in there with nothing."

"I knew you could handle it," Dural replied.

Cai looked at me, then said, "And that's why you're going to need us to handle the next step, too."

Dural slowed the car at a light and cracked her neck, irritated.

"What next step?"

"The books are filled with code," I said. "It won't be easy to extract. But we have a way to do it. Give us some time, seven, maybe six hours; we'll extract the code and hand it to you."

Dural laughed. "How nice of you. And for nothing in return?"

"We'll make a deal," Cai said.

Dural started the car again, eased it onto a highway entrance ramp.

"We will get you the code in return for getting my associate out of the detention center. But to crack this thing, we'll need all the files Naya stole from Nigeria. It's the only way to do it."

"That's a big ask," Dural said. "Those are quite valuable."

"So are we," I said.

Dural smiled.

9. TUNDE

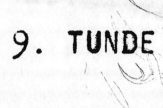

My friends, it was time to build again!

Even though Rex had provided me with very little information regarding the books I was to build a scanner for, I knew the basic properties of how a scanner worked. It was a relatively simple device, one that dated back much earlier than I believe most people assume. There were machines that performed a similar function in the late 1950s, *walahi!*

While I very much would have enjoyed building a scanner that improved upon the existing technology—the few scanners I have taken apart displayed a ridiculous number of engineering faults—there would not be enough time.

I hung up my phone and walked into the kitchen. Rodger Dodger was there, snacking on bites of chocolate cake she had taken from the fridge. She gave me a wave and offered me a piece of the chocolate cake.

"Thank you," I told her, "but something has come up."

"With Painted Wolf?" Rodger Dodger asked.

"Yes," I replied. "I need to build something to help her."

Rodger Dodger nodded. "Excellent, what?"

I will tell you, my friends, I was a little hesitant to answer. It was not that I believed Rodger Dodger would not be capable of helping me but more of my concern about involving her. I knew that I was a young man, but this girl was merely twelve! Clearly, these thoughts were being telegraphed via my expressions because Rodger Dodger jumped up on the kitchen counter and said:

"I know I'm not an engineer or anything. I can't do what you do or what Rex or Wolf does, but I'm not afraid to try anything. I never back down from a challenge, and I've been punching above my weight my entire life. I can help you, Tunde. Just tell me what to do and I'll give it my best shot. What are we building?"

I dey bow na dis girl!

I described the situation to Rodger Dodger. She listened intently. Then I told her some of the materials that I would need to make the scanner. As I saw it, we could easily scavenge materials from various computers and other scanning equipment. But to effectively scan fifteen books that had hundreds of pages each would involve some very powerful machinery. It would need to be industrial.

"I can try to get you whatever you need," Rodger Dodger said, "but most of the stores won't be open right now. We're going to have to scavenge stuff."

"I love to scavenge stuff," I replied. "Scavenged stuff is the best stuff."

Rodger Dodger found some paper and several pencils in the bedroom, and we spread out multiple sheets across the table. I proceeded to sketch some ideas out. My first thought was to use a "drum" at the center of the machine. It would be, essentially, a wide wheel over which the book was placed. The biggest trouble in scanning through so many books is that they are bound. Traditionally that means scanning a page, picking up the book, turning the page, and then scanning again. A laborious process! But with a drum, the pages turn as the drum turns.

Considering the materials we would have available to us, I came up with quite an ingenious idea (if I do say so myself). First was the scanning mechanism. We chose to go with high-speed, high-definition digital cameras placed above and at an angle over the book. The book itself would be laid across the drum, with the covers held fast. Then a specialized "page flipper" (that is what we dubbed it) would flip the pages as fast as possible. Turning the drum seemed a bit clumsy, so this little device resembled fingers and would flick the pages properly.

Hence, it was an automatic flick-book flicker!

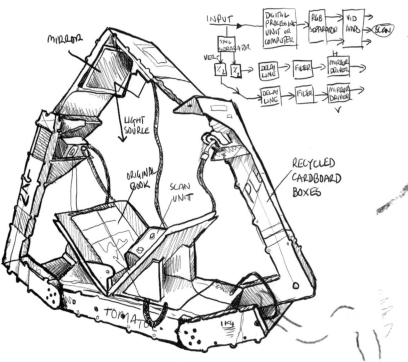

Tunde's scanner

Once the pages were photographed, the images would be fed to a computer to be processed. The program on the computer would coordinate real-time 3-D recognition and high-accuracy restoration of a flat document image. Whatever program Rex designed, it would do the rest.

On paper, it looked very simple. All we needed was the parts.

I asked Rodger Dodger how she felt about the scanner.

"I think it's going to be killer," she said. "Let's start right now."

That, my friends, was exactly when there was a knock at the apartment door.

9.1

I turned immediately to Rodger Dodger.

She shrugged and shook her head, indicating to me that she was not sure who was at the door. This was a dramatic moment. I did not know if the knock was merely a mistake or perhaps it signaled the arrival of the police. Regardless, I wanted to stay mute—we needed to pretend the apartment was empty.

And yet, still more knocks came.

"This is a problem," I whispered to Rodger Dodger, both of us frozen.

Rodger Dodger nodded.

"What do we do?" I whispered.

"Wait till they go away," Rodger Dodger suggested.

"We're not going away."

The voice came from the other side of the front door. It was the voice of a young woman, and it was not familiar to me. She had an accent that sounded, to my relatively untrained ears, to be South American.

The voice continued: "We know you're in there, Tunde Oni. Come on and open the door. This is important."

"This is crazy," I whispered to Rodger Dodger.

I did not know what to do. Rex, Cai, and I had experienced so many different attempted traps over the past few weeks that I was not sure I could trust my own shadow! And yet, the voice on the other side of the door did not seem threatening.

"Please, Tunde," the voice said. "There isn't much time. We need your help."

My friends, this was getting even more confusing.

I stood and approached the front door cautiously. As I did so, Rodger Dodger opened one of the kitchen windows. She signaled to a patio outside, one that we might utilize if we needed to make a hasty escape.

I stopped a foot from the front door.

"How can I help you?" I asked the voice on the other side.

"We have the same goal."

"And what is that?" I asked.

"Stopping Kiran Biswas."

I do not know why I trusted that voice, but there was such sincerity in the way she spoke those words, such determination, that I could not ignore her. As I opened the door, Rodger Dodger made an expression I imagine someone makes when they are about to be run down by a *danfo*. I nodded to her in an attempt to calm her concerns, but I will admit that I still had many of my own.

I unlocked the door and opened it to find something very unexpected.

The three young people that had been following us in

Beijing were now standing in the apartment hallway. My friends, my instincts had been right!

They *were* trailing us, but not for the reasons I had assumed.

"My name is Javiera," the girl I had been speaking with said. "I am from Peru."

She was around my age, with long, dark, braided hair. Javiera had on high-top sneakers and wore a lot of those multicolored rubber bracelets. I noticed that one of them said: <EAT.SLEEP.CODE>. Rex would have been proud.

"Can we come inside?" Javiera asked.

I looked over at the other two young people. An Asian girl of a similar age to Rodger Dodger and a tall, rail-thin, and very pale teenaged boy who wore a beanie.

The younger girl said, "I'm Stella. From Detroit."

"And I am Ivan. From Noril'sk," the boy said in a thick Russian accent.

"Javiera, Stella, Ivan," I said. "Welcome."

9.2

"We're called ULTRA," Javiera said.

She, Stella, and Ivan settled into the apartment, taking seats on the couch across from me. Rodger Dodger walked in from the kitchen and stood behind me. She was quite anxious still; years of hiding will do that to a person.

Looking at the members of ULTRA, I tried to approach the situation as Cai might have. What would she have done? How could I determine that these young people were truly who they said they were? I cogitated on that for a few moments before I turned to Rodger Dodger and said, "They say they are here to help us."

"We are," Javiera said. "We're like you. Like the LODGE."

"I apologize if I appear quite suspicious," I said, "but if you truly know us and know what it is we do, you will understand."

"We have proof," Javiera said. "Here."

She pulled a tablet computer from her bag and handed it to me. On the screen was the forum on our LODGE site. It was open to a user account page. There was a photo of Javiera beside her username and join date. The date was twelve months ago. She had posted 210 times in the forums.

"I joined just before Ivan and a couple months after Stella," Javiera said.

She reached over and flicked through several tabs showing me each of their LODGE site user account pages, each with a photo and their join date. It was clear that they were frequent users of the site long before the GAME.

Javiera continued: "You've probably never heard of us, but we've been fans of the LODGE for a long time. We like to think of ourselves as being on your team. I'm a coder, like Rex. Stella is an engineer like you, and Ivan is a crypto-linguist. We saw what happened to Rex after the Game. After what happened during Zero Hero, I knew Rex must have been framed. We did some research, followed the clues, and formed our own little group. We're actually here 'cause we need your help."

"To do what?" I asked. "Things are a bit complicated right now."

Stella said, "While you've been following Kiran's business interests in Nigeria, India, and now China, we've tracked them through Germany and Greece. And we've found that there is a lab in Mexico City, one that we believe holds the keys to a virus Kiran is building."

"But we have already found this virus," I said. "It is here in China."

Stella looked to Javiera.

Javiera asked me, "What's this virus do?"

"I have not studied it myself," I said. "But Rex says it impacts the banking systems; it is designed to bring down economies. We suspect this is what Kiran has called Shiva, his plan to reorder the world."

"We know of Shiva," Stella said. "But that is not the virus we're after."

Now it was my turn to be surprised. "What do you mean?"

Javiera pulled her cell phone from her purse. She did a quick search and then held up her cell so I could see the screen. On it was an image of the Indian god Shiva, the destroyer and transformer. He was seated in the lotus position, legs crossed, on a tiger pelt. His arms were raised and he held various objects.

"Do you see?" Javiera asked. "He has four arms."

This was true; the depiction of Shiva had four arms.

"Each one is a virus," Ivan said. "We have identified two of them. One was in Kiran's Greek lab. It was designed to affect communications. The virus we discovered in Germany was built to attack security systems. You say the one here in China is for banking. Those are three of Lord Shiva's arms. The fourth, the final one, is in Mexico City. We believe it targets the root servers that connect the Internet."

"Root servers?" I asked.

"The Internet isn't a big, whole system," Javiera said. "It is a whole bunch of tiny systems linked up together. There are hundreds of thousands of tiny Internets that are linked. They communicate with each other via the root servers. If someone takes those offline, it will effectively cut off all the tiny Internets. That sort of thing can be fixed, of course, but not before Kiran has introduced his next move."

"Rama," I said, recalling the program.

"Yes," Javiera said. "That is why we need to stop him now."

"You seem to have figured all of this out," I said. "I applaud you for that. We certainly need as much help as possible in thwarting Kiran. But what is it that you need from me? Why come all the way from Mexico to China?"

"We can't get into the Mexico City lab," Stella said. "We've been running surveillance on it, and it's crazy well protected. We came to you 'cause we need ideas, and we thought that joining forces, the LODGE and ULTRA together, we'd be more effective. We can arrange a flight as soon as tomorrow morning, if you'll join us."

I stood up, feeling the need to stretch my limbs. Rodger Dodger and I were in the middle of a project that I could not abandon. I glanced into the kitchen and saw the plans for the scanner on the table. Even though ULTRA had come to me, had followed us halfway around the globe, their mission would need to wait. I had to build the scanner, bring down Terminal, and clear Mr. Zhang first.

Using my cell, I snapped photos of the LODGE site user account pages Javiera had shown me and I sent them to Cai and Rex. I wanted them to weigh in on this situation before I made a decision. In my text, I wrote, *I have found some friends. They want to join forces.*

I received a response from Cai first.

What is your reading on them, Tunde? she asked.

I believe they are honest, I texted. *And I think they will be helpful.*

91

Two

Hell, yes ☺, Rex texted. *Original fans!*

Cai was more tempered. *We can give them a shot*, she said. *But, Tunde, please be cautious in what you share with them. You are able to read people, trust your gut on this. We will see you soon.*

Bolstered by the compliment and confidence, I turned back to ULTRA.

"Okay," I said. "We can work together."

Ivan clapped; Stella high-fived Javiera.

"But," I continued as their expressions shifted to worry, "I would appreciate some extra hands to complete my work here in China. ULTRA and the LODGE will team up, but our work starts here. Now."

10. CAI

5 DAYS UNTIL SHIVA

Rex, Teo, and I spent the rest of the day at the opera house.

When we arrived back, we unloaded the flip-books, and Dural and the other Terminal members began to look through them. I worried momentarily that they'd start piecing the code together right away, but that didn't happen. They grew bored and restless and decided to go out for a noodle run. Teo offered to go with them to bring us some food. Rex seemed upset by the thought, but he agreed.

Though they had guards placed outside the dressing room door, Rex and I had a moment to talk about our plan and **unpack everything** that had happened. I found an old boom box on a shelf in the corner and turned it up. We had to hope the Chinese hip-hop was loud enough to drown out our conversation from the guards' prying ears and any microphones Terminal had planted in the room.

"So what do you think of this ULTRA thing?" Rex asked.

"Even though I'm cautious, I think it could be good," I said.

"I dig it," Rex said. "More hands to help."

Then, switching gears, he said, "So Tunde will have the scanner in the next couple hours. We'll have to find a way for him to bring it by surreptitiously. In the meantime, we should dig into the data Naya stole. See what we've got."

I said, "Another long day ahead."

Rex rubbed his forehead, eyes clenched tight.

"You okay?" I asked him.

I put my hand on his shoulder, and just the weight of it made him sigh. "Yeah," he said, turning to me, those dark eyes filled with exhaustion. "Just stressed out. This whole thing with Teo . . . I just need him to come around."

"He will."

I was confident that we would convince him. Rex had spent so long looking for his brother and it had paid off. But not the way he'd figured. WALKABOUT didn't find Teo; Teo effectively revealed himself. I knew it could have been Terminal related—given what we knew, there was no doubt that Teo had ulterior motives. If he wasn't trying to help Terminal, his emergence was related to his quest to stop Kiran. And yet, watching Teo with Rex, it was clear that Teo had a deep love for his brother. Teo was in a tough spot, but I had no doubt he'd make the right choice.

"Teo can be stubborn," Rex said. "He thinks only of the end goal. I'm worried that when he figures out what we're doing, how we're changing the code, he's going to tip Terminal off. He'll reveal our hand."

"We won't let him."

"Teo's clever. He'll figure it out."

I leaned in and hugged Rex. Resting my head on his shoulder, I said, "Teo listens to you. Even though he disagrees with the way we're doing things, he understands that we ultimately want the same thing."

A lump rose in my throat as I spoke.

"This is our last chance to get my father out," I said. "If anything goes wrong, my father will likely never see the outside of a prison. Worse, the world is going to pay for our mistakes. Kiran runs Shiva, Terminal uses Naya's data to bring down the banks, we're looking at a total system collapse, and we're the only things standing in its way. I just hope we're up for this."

"Of course we are," Rex said, pulling back so we could look eye to eye.

"We're dealing with so many unpredictable factors and—"

"And I have every ounce of faith in you. After the Game, it became clearer to me than ever that all of my actions, our actions, have consequences—even the smallest choices. I got my parents deported. I got us into trouble with WALKABOUT. But I know what we need to do, and I'm going to follow your lead in getting it done."

"I appreciate that. Just hope I can deliver."

"You've got this. It's brilliant." Then, looking away with a sigh, Rex said, "It's Teo I'm concerned about."

"His intentions are good—"

"But what we've learned about him, the deception, the anger, I don't have the same faith in him that I had before. Feels like for two years I've deceived myself, made up this story of who Teo really was. That's all come **crumbling down**. Truth is, he was probably just as unpredictable before he ran off. I was a kid, he was my big brother, I didn't see what a jerk he was."

"Don't say that," I said. "Teo's family. No matter what choices he's made in the past, you have to believe that he's going to do the right thing now."

"I want to think that's true."

"You're trusting me with the fate of the world." I smiled. "I hope you can trust me on this as well; Teo's going to come through. He's complicated and he'll put up a fight, but in the end, he'll make the right choice."

"Always the optimist," Rex said.

"No," I replied, "Tunde's the optimist. I'm the realist."

Rex smiled and then kissed my forehead sweetly.

"Let's get to work," he said.

10.1

We spent the next six hours figuring out the code.

Teo came back with Dural, Naya, and the other Terminal members shortly after Rex and I had begun. Dural and everyone else went to another room to eat. Teo was determined to help us look through the flip-books. He wanted to know what Kiran was hiding.

Rex and I had to walk a very careful tightrope.

"Maybe you can start with this one," Rex told his brother as he handed him one of the volumes. "Seems to me the code relates more to your interests. Thought I saw something in there about bio storage programs."

Teo took the book, settled into a small leather couch in the corner of the room, and started to scan through the code. He was like Rex in that when he was absorbed with what he was doing, he was largely oblivious to everything else going on around him. While Rex and I talked, Teo kept his eyes glued to the pages, his expression twisted into a concentrated scowl.

"He's gone deep," Rex said, glancing over at Teo.

"Reminds me of you," I said.

"Yeah, but I look better when I'm thinking."

Because we didn't have the time to go through the flip-books one by one and catch every small detail, we had to come up with another way to alter the code—and do it in a manner that didn't tip Terminal off.

That meant rather than altering it, we would have to insert something else into the code—a sort of "trapdoor" that would be hidden from Terminal but would open when the virus was eventually run.

After two hours of near silence, Teo eventually fell asleep on the couch.

As he snored, Rex went into the zone to develop the sabotage code. Just like at the Game, he coded best solo. Sitting in one corner of the room, removed from other thoughts and concerns, he focused himself entirely on the job at hand. I watched as **he wrote furiously**, going through page after page.

After an hour, he walked over to me with a stack of papers. Rex sat with an exhausted sigh.

"Okay," he said, "here's the deal. This is just the first bit of code, but we can get started with it. My handwriting's terrible; can you transfer this onto the corners of the flip-books?"

"Sure," I said. "What's it do exactly?"

"I'm guessing Terminal wants to steal this virus and run it after Kiran takes down the system. That way, they can swoop in right before Rama and steal whatever they can get their hands on. This code we're adding in, it **rewrites the original** virus and then exposes whoever runs it. Not only does it effectively render the virus useless, though they won't know that, but it will also reveal all of Terminal's dirty secrets."

"How?"

"Through a back door program like the one I installed in WALKABOUT 2.0. When the program's run, it'll open, and everything Terminal keeps hidden on their servers will be exposed to the authorities. Should be seamless, so long as they don't find it. And that will come down to our skill at hiding it."

"My handwriting?" I asked.

"In part."

I took the notes Rex had made on scrap paper and wrote the code by hand in the corners of the flip-book pages. It took me a long time, but I was able to closely match the font, case, and size of the print in the flip-books with a pen.

Not perfect, but I assumed it'd be good enough for Tunde's scanner.

Then we numbered each of the books on the spine, one to fifteen, in a way that when scanned properly they'd assemble the code in order. The addition we added was hidden inside the corner text of book number six.

The door to the room opened twenty minutes after we'd finished. It was dusk, and Dural walked in with several cups of steaming hot green tea. Naya looked the worse for wear, with massive bags under her eyes. Teo woke up as the door clicked shut. He rubbed his eyes and glanced over at Rex and me.

"We get it figured out?" Teo asked.

"We figured out how we're going to translate it," I said.

Dural pulled up a chair and sipped her tea.

"So," she said, "tell me how you're going to take the code scattered throughout those books and put it in a form we can utilize."

Rex's cell phone buzzed. It was Tunde.

He answered the phone, spoke briefly, and then turned to Dural.

"The answer to your question," Rex said, "is sitting in the loading bay as we speak."

10.2

Dural escorted us downstairs to the loading bay.

We passed through small groups of actors and acrobats who had arrived early—quite early—to rehearse for that evening's show. If it wasn't already surreal enough walking alongside the leader of Terminal, seeing the actors in their painted guises added a whole new layer. It seemed quite fitting, actually. This whole thing—the scanner, the flip-books— was a charade.

The scanner itself was roughly the size of a large television.

It was a hollow cube. The frame was made of black metal. At its base was a platform with a drum on it. The book would be folded over the drum and locked down. A computer was mounted on one of the upright beams alongside several monitors, and at the top were two high-resolution cameras, aimed down at the drum. It was a simple-looking machine, but I had no doubt it was going to be **insanely effective**. Tunde had never failed to outengineer even the most complicated project.

"It's a scanner," Rex said before Dural could ask. "To take pictures of the flip-book pages and then feed them into the computer. A program will then render the text on the monitor. From what I understand, this should scan two hundred and fifty pages a minute. That means roughly half an hour to get all the flip-books done."

"Who built this for you?" Dural asked.

"A friend," I said.

Dural called Naya over and said, "Make sure there are no tricks here."

Naya, wearing an oversized purse, crouched down beside

the scanner and examined it closely. After she'd gone over it physically, she plugged her cell into the computer via a USB cable and ran several scans. We waited while the scans were completed and Naya turned to Dural.

I watched Naya closely. She was the reason we were here in the first place. If she hadn't stolen the data in Nigeria, my father might not have been in a detention center. I was eager to see her pay for what she'd done. The fact that she came across so confident, so certain Terminal would win, made me furious.

"Surprise, surprise," Naya said. "**It's clean.**"

We carried Tunde's scanner up to the dressing room and placed it on the floor. Then we gathered up the flip-books and stacked them neatly beside the machine. This whole process had to look as professional as possible. We also needed the books in which we'd added handwriting code to not stand out. If Dural, or even Teo, saw the added code, they'd surely suspect something was up.

Dural took a seat on the leather couch beside Naya.

"Let's do this," Dural said, starting a stopwatch app on her cell.

We placed the first book on the drum and turned the system on. When the cameras went live, the monitor flashed on. The pages were loaded into the clip that flipped the pages. With a click of a signal button, the process began. The machine was quiet—the pages were held for a split second before the clip released them and they drifted to the other side of the book. The only audible part of the process was a soft rustling as the pages turned.

As the cameras captured the pages, they were displayed in real time on the monitor. Tunde had designed the system so that it instantly picked out the text on the page, removed it, and reordered it so that we saw the code running vertically down one side of the monitor. When I first noticed it, my heart jumped into my throat. If Dural was watching the monitor closely, she'd see the code flashing by and possibly make out our additions. I wasn't certain how gifted in coding Dural was. Thankfully, as the first book began scanning, a protective measure had popped up on the screen—the code was overlapped with itself several times over. By the time the book was nearing its final pages, the code was a digital jumble on the screen.

Dural noticed that right away.

"What's wrong with the monitor?"

"**A glitch** in the monitor," Rex said as he loaded the next book. "This was a pretty rushed project; not surprised there are a few little gremlins in it. But it's just a display problem—system works fine, don't worry."

"No," Dural said. "Fix it."

"It might take a few—"

"Now," she insisted.

So Rex did. It took him several minutes to dig into the scanner's code. Dural and Naya watched closely as he did. The point of the overlapping had been to ensure that Dural and Naya couldn't suss out what we'd hidden in the code, but clearly it would need to go. We had to **hold our breath** and hope that neither Dural nor Naya would notice the changes.

"There," Rex said. "It's fixed."

The monitor flickered back on, revealing the code running smoothly, unjumbled. My heart was in my throat as Dural gave the signal to start again.

Rex did an excellent job hiding any anxiety he had.

Dural and Naya watched carefully as book after book was loaded and scanned. I sat back and waited, my eyes glued to book number six. Finally, it was time. I tried to calm my nerves as Rex loaded the flip-book into the scanner and turned it on.

For the first few pages, everything went smoothly. The book was scanned, the code appeared on the screen. No one asked any questions or noted the additional numbers and symbols added to this particular book. I was impressed with how cleanly I'd been able to write the code—as the pages flipped by like the beat of a dragonfly's wings, I could hardly tell we'd added anything.

"Hang on," Teo said. "Stop the scan for a minute."

Rex stopped the machine and I held my breath.

Dural leaned forward on the couch and looked at Teo. "What's the matter?"

Teo looked over at Rex. "I think it scanned that last page wrong."

"Okay," Rex said. "We'll just rescan it. Easy."

Teo glanced at me, then turned back to Rex as Rex stopped the scanner, flipped the page back, and got ready to turn it on again. "I'm sorry," Teo said, "I think it's a problem with the camera on the right. Can we just **take a moment** to grab something from out in the hall? This can be fixed easy."

Dural looked concerned. "How long's this going to take?"

"Just a minute, two maybe," Teo said.

"Fine." Dural waved Teo and Rex from the room.

I watched them step outside, the door closed, and I tried to stop the blood from draining from my face. If Teo had discovered we'd hidden the altered code inside the sixth book, everything we'd planned for would be ruined.

Without those files my father would move from the detention center to prison and I would most likely never see him again. The thought made my stomach churn. But not only was my father's fate at stake: If Teo betrayed us, we would be handing Terminal a weapon that would allow them to wreck the international banking system and topple countries with abandon.

11. Rex

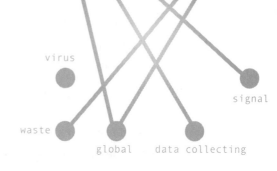

virus

signal

waste

global   data collecting

5 DAYS UNTIL SHIVA

"What the hell are you doing?"

As soon as the door clicked closed behind us, Teo pushed me against the wall.

He was in my face, eyes locked on mine like laser beams.

"I need you to make the right decision here, brother," I said.

Teo shook his head. "What did you do?"

"I'm bringing Terminal down."

Teo let me go and backed up. He was quiet for a moment, chewing over his words. I could tell he wanted to rage at me, to get back in my face and yell.

But he knew that wouldn't work.

I stepped toward him.

"Teo," I said, "Kiran hid a virus in those books. That code we're scanning right now? If it gets out, if Terminal uses it, it will lay waste to the global economy. People will lose everything; they'll suffer. Is that really what you want?"

"They're already suffering, Rex."

"But not like this. This is on a whole other level."

Teo sighed. "What did you do to the code? I saw something in there, a line relating to my bio-computer, only you'd tweaked it. You turned what was a data collecting tool into something that propagated data, a signal."

I nodded.

"What's the signal, Rex?"

"It uses my program WALKABOUT," I said, "the one I built and designed to find you, to mine Terminal's own files and hidden data caches. Instead of attacking the economy, it effectively reroutes Terminal's data to Interpol, the FBI, et cetera, et cetera. If Terminal runs that virus, it will ruin them."

Teo stumbled back hearing that.

He acted like I'd actually punched him in the chest.

"Rex . . . please think about what you're doing. . . ."

"Brother," I said, "you ran out on our family. You abandoned us. And we never gave up looking for you. I devoted the last few years of my life to finding you. I put aside school, a social life, anything a normal teenager does just to find a shred of your existence. I didn't do it 'cause I needed you. I did it because I never stopped believing in you. People said you were part of Terminal, there were rumors you'd gone rogue, but I always trusted that when I found you, you'd be the Teo I remembered."

Teo looked down at his feet, emotion making him blink.

Finally, getting something here . . .

"I knew," I continued, "that when I found you, you'd help me fix this world. You might be angry at how messed up this world is, how screwy and unfair things have gotten, but, in the end, you'll do the right thing."

Teo was silent for a moment before he looked up at me.

"What's the right thing, Rex?"

"Stopping Terminal, clearing Painted Wolf's father, and finding Kiran."

Teo nodded. "How does this help us find Kiran?"

"Tunde has an in with another group," I said. "They've discovered that Kiran has created four viruses. And this one isn't the worst that's out there. If we team up, if we all work together, we can stop Kiran, and, in the process, we can change the world. Please, brother, let's do this the right way. I need you to come in from the cold. Come, be a part of the LODGE."

It was a huge moment.

Here I was, on the other side of the globe from home, asking my brother to join my team. I'd dreamed of this moment for a long time. Seeing him at my side, changing the world together the way we'd talked about as kids. At the same time, this wasn't the Teo I'd grown up with. It hurt me that I couldn't trust him. And I needed to trust him more than anything at that moment.

The door to the dressing room opened. Naya peeked out at us.

"You guys get what you need? Clock's ticking."

"Yeah," I said. "We found it."

"Good," Naya said. "Get your butts back in here."

I walked toward the door and glanced at Teo as I passed him.

He nodded to me and mouthed: *Okay.*

11.1

When we walked back into the room, I could see Cai was struggling to maintain her cool. I walked past her toward the scanner and took her hand and squeezed it. I hoped it was a reassuring squeeze.

Then Teo and I pretended to manipulate one of the cameras.

Teo used a small key-chain screwdriver.

We put on a pretty good show, though I wasn't entirely convinced Dural and Naya would find it persuasive. They had to believe it enough to run the program—once Dural hit that enter button, Terminal would be over.

I stepped away from the scanner.

"We're back in business," I said, and started the scanner.

It whirred back to life, photographing and digitizing pages, as Dural sat back on the couch and watched as the code filled the monitor. I think both Cai and I had our nerves on edge as the scanner wrapped the sixth book. And when it was completed without comment, I tried not to visibly relax.

I loaded up book seven and ran it.

Twenty minutes later, the scanning was done. The last pages were photographed, scanned into the computer, and spat out as a finished code. With the flip-books finished, I walked over to the couch and Dural.

"Do you have a flash drive?" I asked.

Dural chuckled and motioned to Naya.

Naya pulled a chain off her neck; on the end was a flash drive. It reminded me of the one that Teo had left behind, the flash drive I'd worn around my neck for those years he'd been missing. I took the drive from Naya and went back to the scanner. I plugged it in, loaded up the finished code document, and then unplugged the flash drive. Before I handed it to Dural, I paused.

"This," I said, "will give you everything Kiran has."

"What does it do?" Dural asked Naya.

"It's a virus," Naya said. "Taps into the stock market."

"Which stock market?"

"All of them." Naya grinned. "Takes them all down."

Dural seemed very pleased.

As she stood up, Cai turned to face her.

"We have a deal," Cai said. "You will honor it, correct?"

Dural said, "Give me the flash drive."

Cai said, "Make good on your end of the bargain first."

Dural's next-gen phone

"Fine." Dural shrugged, pulled her cell phone out. This phone was something radically different. It wasn't so much that the phone was new, or even that high tech, but it was outfitted with all sorts of additional bits and pieces. My guess was the added tech was to cloak the call, but I have no idea why it wasn't software related. Whatever the case, I assumed it worked. There was no way Dural would be making calls without the ultimate in security on board.

She dialed, then dialed again. Then spoke into the phone.

I couldn't understand what she said. I'm guessing it was in German.

Then she turned to Naya. "I need you to erase some files. They're sending the links to your e-mail address now. Remove all of them, wipe it clean, do it the same way we did the operation in Ecuador. Make the guy a ghost and give a good explanation; leave some misleading bread crumbs like usual."

Naya pulled a laptop from her oversized purse.

I watched Cai as Dural spoke. She was following along with what Dural was doing very carefully. It wasn't just that she was listening intently because this whole thing involved her father. It was that she wanted to know how they were going to get him out—even though she no longer wore the guise of the Painted Wolf, she'd never lose that view of the world.

Naya typed away.

They had it done in a matter of minutes. Naya gave a thumbs-up to Dural, and Dural put the phone on speaker. We could all hear what happened next—a man with a thick Chinese accent said, "Mr. Zhang has been released from custody. He is being escorted by officials to the specified vehicle and will be taken to his home. All charges against him have been dropped. His record is clear."

Dural hung up the phone.

Then she signaled Naya. Naya turned her laptop around so we could see what was on the screen. It was a video, grainy, surveillance, of Cai's father being escorted out of the detention center to a waiting car.

Just before Mr. Zhang got into the car, he turned and looked back at the building, directly at the CCTV camera we were seeing him through, and then nodded his thanks. It was subtle but clearly a message.

Cai turned to Dural. "Thank you," she said.

"A deal's a deal," Dural said. "Now we run it."

I spoke up. "I'm excited to see it."

Dural grinned.

"Of course," she said. "Can't have you all miss the fun."

11.2

We followed Terminal down into the bowels of the opera house.

Dural hurried, excited to see what the virus we'd just given her would do. Naya seemed downright giddy. She literally skipped down the stairs like a kid on Christmas morning.

Teo was the last in line, walking slowly, barely hiding his concern.

I was worried myself.

I knew the code I'd written was decent. I just hoped it would actually function the way I'd designed it to. A lot of that was out of my control. If Terminal decided to target the virus on a particular institution, say a Norwegian bank, instead of letting it propagate naturally across the Internet, then the code might stall out.

Cai kept her eyes on her cell.

Watching the time and waiting for alerts about her dad.

I wasn't the least bit surprised to find they had a fully stocked basement lab down there. They'd transformed a storage room into a high-tech engineering space with rows upon rows of computers and all manner of Frankensteined components in the process of being built or refashioned.

Engineering lab

Dural dragged a rolling chair across the room as the overhead lights flickered on, erasing all the shadows, drenching us in artificial light. Dural sat at one of the computer towers and plugged in the USB. This was the moment, and my heart knew it; it leaped right up into my throat.

On the monitors: Terminal's logo spun to life.

T

You can always tell the bad guys by their logos.

Cold, brutalist, a spinning capital *T* in silver.

Naya looked over at Cai and me. "The LODGE needs something like that. You guys are too stale. Need some flash to mix it up."

Cai said, "We're not about the flash."

Dural logged in, opened the virus files from Tunde's scanners, and then uploaded them to a dark Web Terminal site. From there, Terminal's bot network did its thing, pinging the virus across the globe in a matter of seconds.

My blood pressure was probably through the roof.

As the virus geared up to do its thing, all I could think of was how it could fail. Each step, each computer handshake over the net was an opportunity for something to go wrong. For Dural to catch wind of our trap and sidestep it. I kept eyeing the door, ready to grab Cai and Teo and bolt the second trouble erupted.

Only, that didn't happen.

Incredibly, the intrusion was successful and Terminal was delighted.

Dural leaned back, nodding sagely to herself.

Naya clapped and looked to Cai and me and actually smiled.

"You did good," she said. "Real good . . ."

Despite their excitement, already it was happening: On the monitors the never-ending stream of data was slowing. Several screens began to flash, a warning display showing that the virus had been locked out and the intrusion picked up.

Dural didn't suspect the code at first; she barked over at Naya.

"Our system's lagging. We're getting spotted."

Dural assumed it was their connection, that the bot net was being exposed and blocked by security software. She was wrong. The virus was tagged, little bits of code I embedded that made it easy to pick out. It's complicated but think of it this way: Dural thought Kiran's virus would sneak into these networks like a ghost, but with my tweaks it was barging in like a loud drunk.

And every stumble the virus took, every alarm that sounded on a security server, the authorities were alerted. I knew they'd be knocking down the door to the opera house in a matter of minutes.

When their eyes glued to the screens, I surreptitiously pulled out my cell phone and texted Tunde. I told him the scanner had worked flawlessly, and with the virus unleashed, it would only be minutes before Terminal bit the dust.

Still, until those cops showed up, we were in serious trouble.

The second Dural figured out that running this program was actually exposing Terminal, she would likely do anything she could to stop it. I didn't even want to think about what lengths she'd go to in order to protect her agenda.

We had to get out of there.

Like she was reading my mind, Cai leaned in and whispered:

"We need to leave."

Naya tried her best to fix what she could.

But as more and more of the screens flickered to red— routed by firewalls and security software—even Dural could tell something was very wrong. She spun around to Naya. Naya was going crazy on a keyboard, trying to salvage the assault.

firewalls

exposing Terminal

security software

Cai and Teo left the room first.

They snuck out easily; Dural and Naya were so caught up in what was happening that they didn't even turn around to look.

I needed to be one hundred percent certain that the trick had worked, that my tweaked virus exposed Terminal and that the cops were for sure coming. As I backed up toward the exit, I noticed the screens: Naya was running everything she could to stop the rupture of Terminal data onto the Net. Dural was watching, eyes wide with horror, as Naya was helpless to stop it.

Mission accomplished.

I opened the door as quietly as I could and slipped out.

As I ran down the hallway, the door shutting behind me, I heard Naya rage.

"I don't understand what's happening!"

11.3

Teo, Cai, and I stepped outside to find the street had exploded.

Well, it looked like it had exploded.

The sound of sirens was near deafening as a sea of cop cars, their blue, yellow, and red lights flashing, careened down the street toward the opera house. Cai, Teo, and I quickly slipped into the gathering crowds that had emerged from the buildings to see what all the fuss was about. My code had worked.

Terminal was . . . well, terminated.

The cop cars screeched up the steps of the opera house. The chatter of the watching crowd fell silent as dozens of armed officers raced inside the building. A few performers—acrobats in ornate costumes and a singer with a wild headdress—rushed out of the opera house in a panic.

Cai turned to me and held up her cell phone.

"It's done."

On her cell screen was a text message in Mandarin.

"Good news?" I asked.

Cai said, "My father's home."

I gave her an excited hug, and as we embraced I caught sight of Teo.

He watched the entrance to the opera house with a sad look.

I bumped his shoulder, got his attention.

"You didn't sell them out," I said. "This was all their own doing."

"I'm not upset about that. . . . It's just . . . You're *sure* the LODGE can stop Kiran?"

"I'm positive."

Teo smiled. It was excellent to see his grin brighten again.

Cai nodded, hugging us both.

"Let's go, boys," she said. "You can give each other pep talks later."

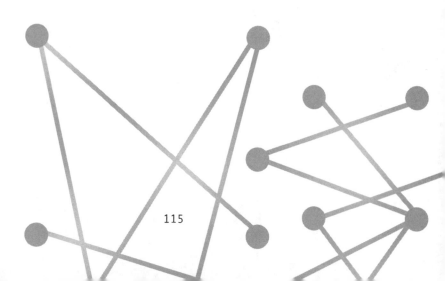

12. TUNDE

5 DAYS UNTIL SHIVA

I ran through the crowd as fast as I could.

I arrived at the opera house just in time to see the most incredible sight!

The very second that I emerged from the crowd was the moment that Dural and Naya and the other Terminal flunkies were led out of the building in handcuffs.

Such excitement! I will admit that I was being quite immoral, rejoicing in the pain of others, but these were bad people and taking some joy in seeing them arrested was surely not a horrible thing. It was, as they say, a long time coming.

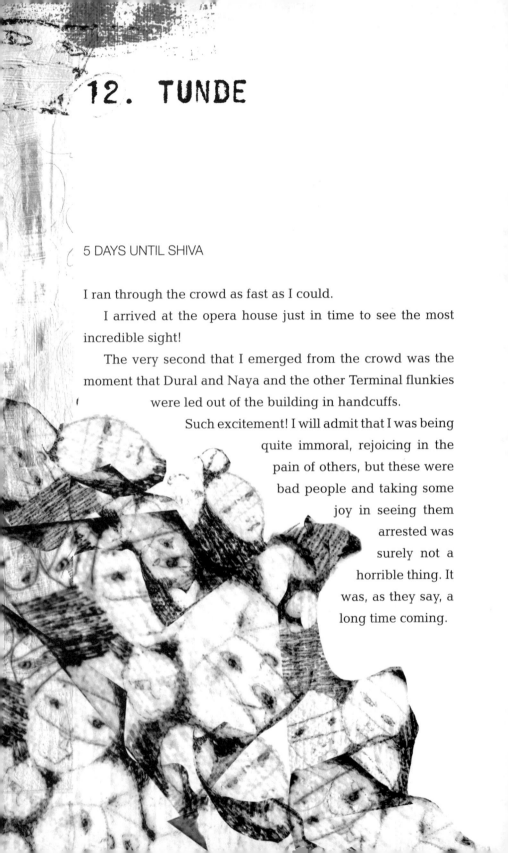

After Dural, Naya, and the rest of Terminal were stuffed individually into the backs of waiting police cars, the doors were slammed shut and the sirens blared again before the cars raced back out into the night. Within seconds, the whole scene had diminished, dwindling to a few scattered police officers attempting to clear the confused crowds of onlookers. That is when I saw Rex, Teo, and Cai walk over to me.

I was so excited to be back with my family again!

I wanted to celebrate our success together. Even though my part in it was quite small, the LODGE had just accomplished a feat that numerous law enforcement agencies were unable to pull off.

I no dey rake but . . . we had taken down Terminal!

There was once a time in my beloved Akika Village when we had to endure the nightly assaults of a panther. I was quite small at the time and have no memory of the events, but my father told me that this animal would descend upon our goats and sheep in the hour just before dawn.

There must have been something quite wrong with the panther because it did not eat what it killed—this beast seemed to enjoy the thrill of the hunt and nothing more. I can tell you that even a decade after the incident with the panther, it is still remembered in my village.

Our best hunter laid traps, but he failed to catch the animal. All of Akika was frightened, and parents, including my own, worried for the safety of their children. If this cat was after sheep today, our elders said, perhaps it will be after people tomorrow.

So hunters were brought in from other, neighboring villages. But even these powerful men failed. The panther, they said, was like a ghost—it could not be caught by traditional

means. My father is not a superstitious man. He knew that this poor panther was certainly ill; the behavior it displayed clearly said as much.

To trap it, my father told me, would require the unexpected.

The method by which the animal was captured was indeed surprising. It was not hunted or baited. Nor was it chased into a net or fed drugged meats. Rather, a medicine woman came up with a novel plan: She told the people of my village to prepare a bed for the big cat! Yes, I know, it does seem quite silly.

But they did it.

Sure enough, this animal was found a day later sleeping in the pile of blankets and rugs they had laid out for it. The hunters crept upon the sleeping cat and tossed a net over it as it was snoring.

Once the big cat was caught, the medicine woman discovered that it had an abscessed tooth. This was, she told the village, certainly the reason why the animal was behaving so strangely. While the panther was in a drugged state, the medicine woman pulled the troublesome tooth. The next morning, the big cat was transported to a zoo in the southwest of Naija-land.

My friends, I think it is obvious why I told you this story.

The LODGE had done the same thing as the old medicine woman from my village—we had captured a rampaging beast that even the best hunters could not track down and we had defanged it. We had done this by tempting Terminal into a state of trust. We gave them what they wanted, and it bit them in the end.

Even though it is not in my nature to celebrate the misery of others, even if they are truly awful people like the general, I was happy to arrive at the front of the opera house just seconds before Dural, Naya, and the rest of Terminal were shuttled into the back of the waiting police cruisers.

My friends, right there in front of the opera house we had a group hug!

A LODGE hug to celebrate a momentous victory.

Afterward, Teo approached me and put out his hand.

I shook it gladly, though I will admit that I was still quite wary of him, considering all that we had learned. I did not want to alarm Rex or insult him, but it would take more than just helping us expose Terminal for me to truly trust Teo.

"Thank you," Teo said. "The scanner was killer. Brilliant."

"I could not have done it without help," I said.

Then, turning to Rex and Cai, I added: "There are some people you need to meet."

12.1

The introduction took place on the roof of an antiquated building.

A cab took Cai, Rex, Teo, and me to the Beijing Ancient Observatory, a massive stone building that stood out in the midst of so many modern, soaring skyscrapers.

On the ride over, Cai asked, "Can you tell us any more about ULTRA?"

"Yes," I said. "But I think it is best for you to meet them for yourselves."

At the observatory, we took an elevator to the roof, where there was an exhibit of ancient Chinese telescopes and other instruments for stargazing. Most of them were installed during the Ming dynasty, over six hundred years ago. They were beautiful. On the rooftop, we looked over the sextant and theodolite, but Rex and Cai were too eager to meet my "mysterious" acquaintances to marvel at the old objects. I would have loved to spend a few minutes longer with the ancient technology, but, dear friends, it was simply not the time.

I made a vow to come back again!

"Rex Huerta!"

Rex, Cai, and Teo spun around as though someone had just fired a cannon over their heads. The cannon, however, was merely Javiera. She stepped out onto the roof alongside Stella and Ivan.

Seeing them, both Rex and Cai looked at me confused.

"Meet my friends," I said.

Javiera introduced the team and their skill sets.

"We call ourselves ULTRA," she then said. "We're big fans of the LODGE, and we're after the same thing you are—finding a way to stop Kiran from breaking the world. We've discovered Kiran's next step. There's a black box lab in Mexico City. We need your help to get inside. We've been talking to Tunde, and we think we're in the final stretch of this thing—we bring down that Mexico City lab and we can cripple Kiran's ability to move forward. He'll be scrambling."

"I like the sound of that," Teo said as he shook hands with Javiera.

"What do you need us to do?" Cai asked.

"Come to Mexico City. Help us breach the lab," Ivan said. "We were able to lose Kiran's tail a few cities back. We've been in so many that, frankly, I can't remember where it was. And while he might be expecting us to approach his Mexico City lab, he certainly won't expect us together."

"So what's in this Mexico City lab?" Rex asked.

Stella spoke next. "We believe it houses the core of his brain trust," she said. "All the folks who worked at the lab here in Beijing, they've gone to Mexico City. I think Kiran is scrabbling to get all his people in line. These folks are his closest advisers, the architects of the Shiva and Rama programs."

Rex nodded. "Sounds like he's been backed into a corner."

Cai said, "I wouldn't make any assumptions. Perhaps he's backed into a corner, or perhaps he just wants us to think he is. If you're right and he's getting desperate, that only means he'll be more dangerous to deal with. He might get impulsive."

"Classic two-player, zero-sum game," Ivan said. "Very tricky."

Cai called a huddle.

Rex, Teo, and I joined her beneath one of the ancient artifacts lining the roof. We could look down at the roiling city below; the air was muggy and thick and all the lights of the passing cars seemed refracted in a million pieces. The sky was very dark, and I could not see any stars. It was as though we were inside a tunnel.

"This seems almost too good to be true," Rex said.

"Because it's Mexico City?" Cai asked.

"That," Rex said, "and the fact that this ULTRA group seems almost too perfectly aligned with our own. I mean Ivan has the game theory lingo, Stella's an engineer, and Javiera just happens to be a coding prodigy. Sounds familiar, right?"

"You suggesting this is a trap?" Teo asked.

"I'm suggesting there's something going on here," Rex said. "How is it that this ULTRA team has been after Kiran, mirroring our movements, and we haven't heard a single peep about it?"

"They might not be the only ones," I added.

That got everyone thinking for a few quiet seconds.

"I don't think this is something Kiran came up with," Cai responded.

"My friends," I said, "I can assure you they are good people, incredibly smart, and dedicated to this cause. When I suggested that there might be other teams like them, I was in no way suggesting that as a *bad thing*."

"So it's what, then?" Rex asked.

"What we are seeing," I said, "might be something quite incredible. Groups of young people like us, young people like the members of ULTRA who have read our work and are now following the same leads that we are. Young people who have discovered what Kiran is attempting and are dedicated to stopping him. I think this could be the beginning, *omo*."

"Beginning of what?" Teo asked.

I gave my compatriots a winning smile.

"A truly inspirational partnership," I said.

Turning away, Rex called to ULTRA, "Okay, we're in."

"Great." Javiera grinned. "When can we leave?"

13. CAI

"Next available flight to Mexico City isn't until tomorrow morning," Ivan said, looking at his cell. "It's an early flight."

"Excellent," Tunde said. "But I am sure it is going to be quite pricey."

Javiera pulled out her cell.

"I got this."

Her hands moved quickly over the surface of her cell, typing even faster than I can. I watched her expression as she swiped across screens and filled in text.

While everything was being set up, I had to admit I was feeling anxious to see my parents. I'd only been in China a few days and already we were leaving again.

I understood Rex's caution about ULTRA, but I believed Tunde was right. It didn't change the fact that we had to focus on the plan at hand—whatever was happening out in the larger world, we needed to keep our sights on Kiran.

I was only an hour from my house, and my father had been released after a terrifying stretch behind bars. I knew that my time away, my lies and my deceptions, had harmed them. I'd spent weeks lying to my mother, I'd put my father in harm's way, and, even though I hadn't shown it to Rex and Tunde,

I desperately needed closure with my parents. I wanted to apologize and make everything right again. And I wasn't going to leave China until I had.

Javiera looked up at us and put her cell in her pocket.

"We have seven tickets to Mexico City at seven a.m. tomorrow," she said. "Couldn't get us in first or business class, sorry. And we're not all together. But it's a flight and it's free."

Rex nodded, impressed with her work.

I thanked Javiera for securing the tickets.

"No, thank you," Javiera replied. "We're just thrilled to be working with you."

"Huge honor," Ivan said.

We all turned and looked down at the city beneath the planetarium.

"Well, we've had quite a night," Rex said. "What's next?"

Tunde said, "I do not know about you all, but I am exhausted."

"We need to move," Teo replied. "Knowing Terminal, I'm sure they're not exactly going to admit what they've done. They're going to blame someone, anyone, else. They're probably trying to set up the LODGE as we speak."

"And that means the authorities," I said.

"We have a **safe house** we crash at nearby," Stella said. "But it's small, can barely fit the three of us. I hate to say it, but do you guys have any place to go?"

Teo said, "We can go to my apartment, but it's all the way across town."

I already knew where we needed to go.

"I have a place," I said.

13.1

My mother answered the door to our apartment and nearly fainted.

I should have warned her that I was coming home, but I didn't want to ruin the surprise. Instead, I practically gave my poor mother a heart attack. She embraced me and then held me at arm's length so she could look in my eyes.

"Cai," she said, breathless, "what has happened?"

"I want to **explain everything**," I said. "Tell me Father is okay."

"He's here, just got home only a few hours ago."

I looked around my mother's shoulders briefly to see if I could spy him sitting in his favorite chair or standing in the doorway to the kitchen, but I didn't see him.

"Cai, tell me what is going on. I don't understand any of this."

"Mom," I said, locking my eyes on hers, "I promise you I will explain everything that has happened, but first, I need to introduce you to some friends of mine. They need a place to stay for the night and . . ."

My mother glanced past me to see Rex, who waved sheepishly; Tunde, who was grinning ear to ear; and Teo, hanging back behind the other guys.

"All of them?" my mother asked, shocked.

"They'd happily sleep on the living room floor," I said.

"I haven't been shopping yet this week."

"They'll be fine," I said. "Don't worry about it."

My mother considered the request for a moment, examining the people standing out in her hallway, before opening the door wider and bowing to invite them inside. I went first and Tunde followed quickly after.

He stepped into the room and shook my mother's hand vigorously.

"My name is Tunde Oni. I am from Akika Village in Nigeria. It is truly an honor to meet you, Mrs. Zhang," he said. "Your daughter has saved my life on several occasions. I assure you that I am not being factitious. You will never believe the adventures that we—"

I stepped in and interrupted Tunde. He understood, gave my mother another brisk handshake, and stepped aside.

Rex was next. He nodded to my mom and did something of a bow. I could tell he wasn't sure what the right move was, but he was trying what he'd seen other Chinese people do. He was awkward. It was cute.

"I'm Rex," he said.

"It is very nice to meet you, Rex," my mother said. "Welcome."

Teo was next. He introduced himself in Mandarin, and my mother was quite impressed. By the time we'd gone through introductions and everyone was standing in my family's rather small apartment living room, my father emerged from his bedroom. He was wearing jeans and a soft button-up shirt, the sort of clothing he put on when he was relaxing at home. While he seemed quite surprised to see three foreigners standing in his apartment, he appeared most stunned to see me there.

I ran over to him and embraced him.

"I don't know what to say," I began. "I'm just glad it's finally over."

"How on Earth did you pull it off?"

I shook my head, tears already forming. "It wasn't easy."

My father looked at me, astonished. "I thought **I was lost.** I was sure they'd throw the book at me and I'd never see you or your mother again. It was terrifying. And then you walk in from out of nowhere. Seeing you there, I was worried. Never in a million years did I think you'd actually pull it off."

"I couldn't have done it without my friends," I said.

"They have my eternal gratitude."

After a moment's silence, my father said,

"Your mother . . ."

I knew what my father was going to say. He was clearly deeply concerned about my mother. She'd been kept in the dark about everything—my initial travels to the Game, my father's trip to Nigeria, his incarceration—and now it was time to let her in. There was no way I was going to leave again without telling her. More than that, I wanted her to know what we were doing. I knew she'd worry. But I also wanted her to appreciate what we were doing. **I wanted her to be proud of me.**

I separated from my father and took him by the hand to the couch.

I had him sit beside my mother while Rex, Tunde, and Teo sat on the floor as though they were students at an assembly.

Then, the only one standing, I turned to my parents.

"I am Painted Wolf," I said.

13.2

I had divulged the will of heaven.

In China, that's an expression that means: I let the cat out of the bag. My father, of course, was not surprised. My mother, however, was shocked. She turned to my father, her eyes wide, and demanded to know what he knew and how he knew it. My father demurred and turned my mother's attention back to me.

"Mother, you're not going to believe what I'm about to tell you," I said. "But I need you **to know the truth**. Not because I need to get it off my chest, though keeping the truth from you has been very difficult, but because we're going to need your help."

My mother leaned forward, with hands clasped together, and listened.

I began to tell our story where it truly started, with Painted Wolf. I explained to my mother how I became my alter ego. What I was attempting to do. I didn't get into the level of danger involved or the risk that I'd taken, but I made clear how devoted to the cause I was. Then I explained how I met the LODGE.

Rex and Tunde told their stories. Teo added where he could. He was not shy about his "disappearance" and explained how he'd left his stable, happy life behind to try to shake things up. This led to Terminal and, in turn, to Rex's creation of WALKABOUT. Tunde talked about the Game. I talked about Kiran and how we'd uncovered his plans with Shiva and Rama. It was so good to get the whole story off my chest that I took the time to go into great detail—how we escaped authorities in New York, how we defeated General Iyabo while Rex was in India surveilling Kiran from "behind enemy lines," and how we wound up bringing down Terminal ourselves. The action, my illness in Akika Village, I told my mother and father about all of it—well, everything except how Rex and I had kissed. Several times.

When we finished, I realized we'd been talking nonstop for an hour.

My father looked exhausted; he'd been there for some of it and had experienced firsthand the chaos and the confusion.

My mother, however, was on the edge of the couch, eyes locked on mine. She was enthralled.

With my throat dry, I sat down beside her on the couch.

She took my hands in hers and said, "I am very proud of you. You are so selfless, so clever, so kind, and so very, very brave. I could never have accomplished half the things that you've done in only a couple of weeks. But . . . you lied to me, and I'm very upset about that."

A lump formed in my throat. I knew that it wouldn't be as easy as me just telling my mother the whole story and her accepting it. That would have been too easy. From the moment I'd left the house for my first mission as Painted Wolf, I understood that there'd come a time when I'd have to account for my lies, to the deception that I'd caused, and face my mother's disappointment.

"I'm sorry, Mother," I said, "but it was the right thing to do."

"Why didn't you trust me?"

"I did, but . . . I knew you would try to stop me."

"I'm your mother," she said, crying now. "Of course I would have."

"Mother," I said, "I need for you to trust me and trust that my friends will take care of me. We've been around the globe, and they've kept me safe the whole time. **We're strong** together, and we still have much to do."

My mother's hands tightened on my shoulders.

A moment passed between us, and we both came to a silent though mutual understanding—she would not be able to keep me safe at home and I would not be able to keep my activities a secret from her.

"Come," my mother said. "Your guests look hungry."

13.3

Rex, Tunde, and Teo stayed in the living room, talking to my father, while my mother and I went to the kitchen to prepare a meal.

There was nothing I could have wanted more at that moment.

Once in the kitchen, we were in complete sync, as though the past two weeks hadn't happened. My mother suggested we make hot and sour soup, stir-fried tomatoes with scrambled eggs, *Jing jiang rou si* (a traditional dish of pork in sweet bean sauce), and a pickled meat dish that my father loved.

Surrounded by the smells of the kitchen and the cuisine, I was instantly at ease. My mother and I worked side by side, cutting vegetables and slicing meat, stirring and tasting the broths and sauces. While we'd eaten sparsely during our time in Beijing, a few scattered meals of dumplings and noodles, preparing this comfort food suddenly made me ravenous.

"Father's name is clear," I told my mother. "You don't have to worry."

She washed her hands and then, wiping them dry on a hand towel, turned to me. "He is a good man but he gets too ambitious. He wants more and better for us all the time. There is something of his ego in it, too. But I never thought he'd resort to—"

"It wasn't his fault. He made some deals that looked too good to be true. At the end of the day, they were. Father never broke the law; he just got in over his head. He's free and clear now, Mother. Everything is as it was."

She considered that, knitting her brow, as she filled a bowl of water for the rice. After a moment, she said, "Your friends seem quite nice."

"They're wonderful."

"And the one with unruly hair?"

I was scrambling the eggs and looked down at my whisk. "His name's Rex."

"He's handsome," my mother said.

I knew that I was blushing but kept my head down and my attention focused on the bowl in front of me. "Well, I don't know about that," I said, somewhat quietly, trying not to let any emotion slip into my words, "but he's very smart. He's a coder."

My mother bumped my hip.

"I can tell **he likes you**."

My father brought several folding chairs up from the storage room in the basement, and we all crowded around our small dining table. My parents sat on either side of me, with Rex by my father and Tunde by my mother. My mother seemed entranced by Tunde's stories of life in rural Nigeria, while my father was impressed by Rex's deep knowledge of digital camera programming.

Listening to everyone speak, watching them enjoy the food that my mother and I had prepared, I could not help but think back to the last big meal I'd had. It was in Akika Village with General Iyabo and couldn't have been a more contrasting scene. There, we'd eaten in fear and discomfort, while at my home the air was filled with cheer and the sweet sound of enjoyment. Thinking back on it, I appreciated just how much we'd accomplished. That made my food taste all the better.

"The eggs are delicious," Rex said from across the table.

"Thank you," I said.

"This is truly an incredible meal," Tunde said as he stood, holding his teacup in his hand and raising it for a toast. We all raised our cups as well. "I want to thank our gracious hosts, Mr. and Mrs. Zhang and their amazing daughter. I know that I speak for Rex, Teo, and myself when I say that I could not imagine a finer dinner and a more hospitable place to spend the evening. Truly, deeply, from the bottom of my heart, I want to thank you."

We all clapped. My parents beamed shyly.

It wasn't until after the boys had cleaned up the meal and we'd all had our fifth cup of tea that I realized how exhausted I was. I slept in my bed for the first time in weeks while Rex, Tunde, and Teo slept on the floor near the closet. Tunde and Teo were asleep first, both of them snoring heavily under a pile of duvets. Rex tossed and turned before quietly asking me if I was awake.

I was.

"I've been thinking about this whole crazy thing," Rex whispered. "I've learned so much about myself doing this. I was kind of a brat before, determined to do my thing no matter the costs. I guess you showed me that everything we're doing has so much more reach. It goes way beyond what I expected, and **I'm proud of that.**"

"I didn't teach you," I said. "You discovered it yourself."

"You showed me, though."

Rex carefully got up and crept over to me. He leaned down, kissed me, and then said, "You make me a better person, Cai."

Then he snuck back to the floor and fell asleep.

I watched him sleep for a few minutes, my mind spinning. I thought about our upcoming trip to Mexico City, imagined how we might get inside the final black box lab and make our way past Kiran's finest brain trust members, before my thoughts turned to the future. I wondered: What did my normal look like? Did I even have a normal life? Could I imagine myself going back undercover as Painted Wolf and creeping down air ducts and setting up surveillance cameras on rooftops?

Those thoughts tumbled through my head for a few moments.

However, I smiled before I fell asleep.

"Of course I can," I told myself. "I'll always be Painted Wolf."

PART TWO

INTO THE FUTURE

14. Rex

We left Cai's apartment around four in the morning.

Her parents were awake and sad to be seeing her go so soon.

But they seemed to understand; this thing wasn't over.

Mr. Zhang knew Kiran needed to be stopped and we were the only ones who could do it. We'd freed him. We'd taken down Terminal. Kiran was next.

Meeting Cai's parents was wonderful.

Truth is: I was more anxious when that apartment door opened than I was when I'd hacked into the Game. Running from the police has nothing on the heart-pounding anxiety of meeting your girlfriend's folks. I fully expected her dad to give me the third degree, but they were sweet and, above all, understanding.

The way they reacted, the way they listened, Cai couldn't have had better parents—even though they were protective, they saw her for who she truly is and encouraged her to embrace that inner rebelliousness.

Of course, it only reminded me that I needed to see my parents.

They knew Teo was okay, that I'd found him.

But now they were going to actually see him again.

Mental note: Prepare for some emotional fireworks.

After a last round of good-byes to Cai's parents, we snagged a cab to Beijing Capital International Airport. I wasn't the only one jazzed. Tunde was a talkative ball of nerves. Teo bounced his left knee the entire drive.

"What's first?" I asked the team as we pulled up to our departure gate.

"Reconnaissance," Cai said. "We need eyes on that black box."

"Do we have any idea where Kiran is?" Tunde asked.

"From what I can tell," Teo said, swiping through screens on his cell, "he's gone underground. No social media, no messaging. I saw something from an OndScan account where the company praised the takedown of Terminal and mentioned that Kiran was taking a brief vacation. But that's it."

"Do you think he is in Mexico City?" Tunde asked.

"We'll find out . . . ," I said.

ULTRA met us at the ticketing counter. Javiera, Ivan, and Stella looked exhausted—big bags under their eyes.

Before I could even ask, Javiera said, "We made our safe house, but it was crashed at two a.m. by the cops. We've been up since then, cabs, trains, on foot. I think we're all going to be passed out before the plane even takes off."

"Terminal's down and out," Teo said. "Who do you think got to you?"

"Kiran," Ivan said. "He even sent us a lovely message."

Stella produced a tablet computer from her bag and opened a video message she'd received via an anonymous chat app. She pressed play, and there was our old friend again, wearing only designer clothes and smiling with too-perfect teeth. Even though Kiran looked just as together as always, just as much the guru, there was a heaviness that had sunk into his eyes. A strain. I was happy to think that maybe the LODGE and I had put it there.

"Hey, ULTRA," Kiran said. "I've been hearing rumors that you're running around now with the LODGE. I'm impressed. It's like a superhero team up or something—two groups of incredibly gifted but delusional young people who are under the misguided impression that I'm out to ruin the world. I have some breaking news for you: Terminal is no more. The real bad guys are out of the game, so to speak. Yet I have no doubt that you're not going to abandon your mission. Don't worry. I'll keep making it as entertaining as possible. Say hi to Painted Wolf for me."

The video stopped and went to black.

"I see he isn't any less a jerk than before," I said.

"He's worried," Cai said. "I can read it in his face. He tried to play off Terminal's being arrested as nothing major. But it has him spooked. We have the upper hand right now; if we can hit the black box lab quickly, we'll leave him spinning. And that is exactly where we want him."

While I wasn't as confident as Cai, I got a similar sense.

Tunde, as usual, wasn't as convinced.

"Maybe this is what he wants us to think?" Tunde said. "We cannot be too sure with Kiran. He has surprised us too many times."

Passing through security with no problems felt . . . off.

This shouldn't be this easy.

It took a good half hour, and the whole time I was overly

conscious of my body language and where I was looking. There were numerous Chinese police and military milling about, but for the most part they ignored us; just another round of tourists making their way out of the country. I was stunned. Whatever mojo Kiran had pulled to ghost out our identities made us better than invisible. We could truly hide in plain sight.

An hour later, we were on the plane.

I sat beside Teo and Cai. Tunde joined Javiera and Stella a half-dozen rows behind us. Ivan was consigned to a seat at the back of the plane. He didn't seem to mind; he was eager to sleep for most of the twenty-plus-hour flight ahead.

We didn't talk as the plane taxied and took off.

All of us were lost in thoughts of what was to come next.

I looked out the window at the dizzying expanse of the city.

Cai took my hand and squeezed it.

"So what happens next?" I asked.

"We keep going," Cai replied.

"And after that?"

"Hard to say," she said. "You're assuming it all works out, that we stop Kiran and make everything right. It's hard for me to think more than two steps ahead at this point."

"Well, what are the two steps you see?"

Cai glanced over at Tunde. He'd fallen asleep.

"We get to Mexico City," she said. "There, we'll work with ULTRA to find a way into this last black box lab, and then we see where those clues lead us. If ULTRA is right, we find Kiran and we confront him."

I squeezed Cai's hand. "Easy."

She laughed.

"I can't imagine going back to how things were before all this," I said. "Being in school, sitting at a desk, bored out of my

mind, and then just . . . I don't know if I can sit back and watch the world go by anymore. I feel like I have to be involved now, on every level."

"You were involved before, Rex. You just didn't see it."

"What do you mean? I wasn't racing around the world."

Cai said, "All that coding you did for WALKABOUT, the forums, the sites, the social media, you were everywhere. Maybe you were doing it all from your laptop or your cell phone, but you were doing it. Think about everyone we've met. Even if they didn't know your name or your face, they understood what you were working for. I know what you mean, seeing all this, being exposed to the world, it changes you. But I don't think things are really going to be that different when we get home."

"Doesn't feel that way."

"You'll see." Cai smiled.

14.1

Seven thousand miles and a day and a half later, we were at a café on the corner of Calle Xicotencatl and Ignacio Allende in Mexico City.

Tunde's people, his family, were all safe.

Cai's father was out of jail, his record clear.

I was in the country of my ancestors. Even though I was desperate to see my parents and bring Teo back into the fold, we couldn't make contact with them yet. Kiran's message made it clear we were going to be on his radar soon—if we weren't already. We had to get this done as soon as possible.

Across the street was one of Kiran's black box labs.

Here's where it all goes down, good or bad. . . .

141

Despite the fact that there were seven of us huddled around a café table only one hundred yards away, Cai seemed convinced we didn't stand out. The plaza was crazy crowded, and there were tourists of every stripe around.

The black box lab building was a simple brick affair with very few windows. Those that existed were blacked out. The place resembled a three-story jail more than anything. Because it was so nondescript, getting an idea of what was inside it was going to be particularly tricky.

Good news was: We had more hands than ever.

Cai said, "Plan's simple: If this lab is where the Shiva program will be launched from, we need to see inside it. Since we don't have time to set up a proper surveillance system, we're going to have to wing it. We need to intercept their communications externally and get whatever data internally that we can."

"What're we thinking?" I asked the others.

"I am thinking there is an amazing communications array on that tall building beside the lab," Tunde said, pointing to the roof of an office building. He was right; there was a smorgasbord of satellite dishes and antennae on the roof. Many of the cables leading to and from the array led directly, though surreptitiously, to the black box lab—a clever rerouting to distract potential spies.

Tunde continued: "I may be mistaken, but from what I can see from here, it appears as though this communications array belongs to our friend and his brain trust. If we can tap into it, we can tap into their systems."

"Excellent," I said. "Cai, Ivan, how we feeling?"

"Beautiful," Ivan said.

"Let's do it," I said.

142

Half an hour and fifteen flights of stairs later, we were on the roof of the building next to the black box lab. Tunde and Stella looked over the satellite array and walked us through the details of how they'd gain access to the lab's feed.

It was complicated, and we left Tunde and Stella to figure it out.

Rooftop satellite

Twenty-two minutes later, they had it.

They were able to redirect the busy stream of information coming from the black box lab to a program on Javiera's cell phone. That way she and I could get a look at the stream of data as it zipped up into space and then back down to the rest of the brain trust and Kiran . . . wherever he actually was.

143

What we saw was not pretty.

"They're preparing the fourth virus," Javiera said, eyes on the screen. "All the traffic running in and out of that place is focused on building a system of back doors to let the virus loose. Literally every computer in there is targeted for that one purpose. Kiran's going for broke."

"How about security?" I asked.

"The lab's running 4096-bit RSA encryption, not easy to crack."

Javiera looked up from the screen at the team.

"So maybe we do a side-channel attack with acoustic cryptanalysis," I said. "We turn on some of the microphones inside that place, listen in on the high-pitch frequencies that computers use to decrypt data, and we can hack them."

"Technically possible," Javiera said, "but not doable with our time frame."

"It would take us days to build that sort of setup," Stella added.

"We don't have days," Cai said, hammering it home.

"We know the launch is imminent," Javiera said.

"And we cannot do anything from here?" Tunde asked.

"Not this way," Javiera said, "but . . ."

Then she turned and looked at me.

14.2

It was costume time.

We stopped by a clothing store a few blocks from the black box lab and scored an outfit for me. It was my turn to play the Painted Wolf role.

While Cai was in her full Wolf regalia, all the classic stuff she'd picked up at home, and looked pretty badass in a leather jacket, I wasn't looking nearly so cool.

For me, the dress code was nerdy.

I needed to look as black box brain trust-y as possible— bright colors, a hip jacket, and glasses (outfitted with several cameras, of course). I even put my hair up in a high ponytail and put on a rather effective fake goatee Cai had assembled from her hairpieces. Cai laughed the first time she saw it. I gave her a dirty look and she corrected herself.

"It's cute," she said.

Cute or not, it had to work.

I was going into the lab for some firsthand recon.

Security was crazy tight on the array—the brain trust kids in the Mexico City black box lab had done some insane work keeping their outgoing signal secure. The only way we were going to get meaningful intel on Shiva was from *inside* the lab. And since I'd actually worked in the Kolkata black box lab, I was the best one to go in.

The rest of the crew, the LODGE and ULTRA, waited for me a couple blocks away as I walked over to the black box lab solo. I'll admit: I was nervous.

I hoped my sweat wouldn't loosen the glue on my goatee.

I stepped up to the front door with a tiny earpiece in my left ear.

The LODGE was on the other end.

"There are cameras mounted on the exterior," Cai said to me through the earpiece. "You can defeat the facial recognition software, but you'll need to talk fast. We've confirmed the name of a software engineer inside. He's Carson."

"Carson," I repeated. "I'm on it. No problem."

Truth is: My guts were churning.

I knocked on the front door. It had no doorknob, no peephole. Just a metal door set into a metal frame. There was no answer. So I knocked again. This time, there was a squeal of metal as locks disengaged and the door slid open.

A young woman with oversized glasses stood there staring at me.

"Yes?" she said, irritated.

In Spanish, I said: "So sorry to interrupt, but I need—"

"Do you speak English?" the young woman cut me off.

I put on my best, thickest Mexican accent. "Yes," I said. "I need to talk to Carson. It's very important and concerns what happened in China."

Oversized Glasses looked very confused.

"Um . . ." She wasn't exactly sure how to respond.

I'd caught her off guard. The plan was working.

"You weren't expecting me?" I asked. "No surprise there, considering what's been going on. Tell Carson I'm from the Beijing office. I'm sure you heard about what happened, correct?"

She shook her head.

"You didn't?" I feigned shock. "Well, I really need to talk to Carson now."

The young woman stood there, flustered, unsure of what to do next.

"What is your name?" I asked her.

"Um . . . N-Nicole," she stammered.

"Good, Nicole. Please get me Carson stat."

"I'm afraid that won't be possible," Nicole said, mechanically repeating something she'd probably been trained to say.

"This is a restricted facility, and you'll need authorization to get any farther. If you're really—"

"This lab's been compromised," I interrupted. "It's incredibly important. I need to come in now. You can explain to Kiran why you kept me waiting."

As Nicole waffled, I stepped past her inside.

14.3

I walked out of the heat and into a maelstrom.

"Nicely done," Cai said into my earpiece.

"Bravo," Tunde added.

"Could've been better," Teo said.

"Yeah, yeah," I whispered back. "Now, *shush.*"

ULTRA was right. The Mexico City black box lab certainly looked like Kiran's last-ditch attempt to launch his Shiva and Rama programs.

I think *beehive* is an appropriate description.

The Kolkata black box lab was lightly staffed compared to the crowd I found myself among. There were well over a hundred brain trust prodigies running back and forth, crazily, around the Mexico City lab. And unlike Beijing's clever analog library, this place was packed with computers and servers.

It truly was a hub. If there was another virus like the one we'd intercepted, this would be the place to launch it from.

Nicole scrambled behind me, tugging at my shoulder, trying to get me to listen. "There's procedure that needs to be followed," she continued. "Kiran was very strict about—"

"So is Carson here?" I asked.

"He's in a meeting," Nicole said.

I stopped in the middle of a lobby.

"Then I guess you're going to have to interrupt it," I said. "While you're at it, I'll need a rundown of everything you're doing securitywise. All the software, whatever hardware you have in place."

"I don't have—"

"Can you get it?"

Nicole wasn't sure how to reply.

Finally, she said, "Give me two minutes."

I watched as Nicole headed up a nearby staircase, eyeing me the whole while. I looked at my watch, pretending to be seriously annoyed. As soon as she vanished into an upstairs room, I took a good look around the three-story building. It had an open interior with workstations lining the sides on each floor. Staircases branched up and down, winding around like some M. C. Escher building.

If the architecture wasn't wild enough, the mood of the place was total panic.

And that panic provided me with some cover.

I ducked over to an unoccupied computer terminal in a corner. I couldn't use the passcodes I'd been given in India to log in 'cause that would tip off Kiran something fierce. Instead, I hacked my way in. Took a good thirty seconds, but it didn't take me much longer than that to find hints of what I was looking for.

The Shiva program was indeed inside the lab, but . . .

"You see what I see?" I asked the rest of the team.

I angled my glasses so they could see the screen I was looking at.

On the monitor in front of me was a running log of the black box lab system's programs. They were all piecemeal.

No one program was running by itself; they were all tied into each other like lines in a spider's web.

"I am not sure what it is we are looking at," Tunde said. "Explain it."

"They're running a clever system that's broken up every piece of software associated with Shiva and intertwined it with something else," I whispered. "You pull one piece, you pull them all. But the most important thing is this. . . ."

I pointed to a line of code on the screen.

"Shiva is housed here but launched from somewhere else," I said. "I'm not going to have enough time right now to figure out exactly where that is. We need to come back here and bust this thing wide open."

That's when I noticed Nicole coming down the stairs alongside a guy with spiky hair. He must have been Carson. He didn't look too happy to have been interrupted.

I needed to get out of there quick.

At the same time, I noticed a bank of monitors across from me displaying an OndScan news feed of sorts. On the feed: closed-circuit-TV images of Cai, Tunde, Teo, and me in Beijing. They already had us identified.

I saw Nicole glancing around the room, looking for me as I ducked down low and scrambled toward the front door. A few people noticed me, but they were all in such a rush that I doubted they were really paying that much attention.

I hit the front door and got it open seconds before Nicole and Carson turned toward me. I wasn't sure if they'd seen me duck out, but I'm sure they saw the door closing. I had to run fast.

I scrambled out into the daylight. And tore off the goatee as I ran.

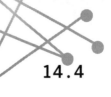

14.4

As I raced across the plaza, I practically yelled into my earpiece.

"They're onto us!"

"Who?!" Tunde asked. "The police?!"

"Kiran, maybe everyone!"

I glanced up at the rooftop and could see Teo, Tunde, Stella, and Javiera grabbing their equipment, shoving it into their pockets.

"Hurry!" I shouted into my cell.

I wasn't sure exactly where we were going but followed Ivan as he ran down the narrow streets bordering the plaza. We dodged traffic, car horns blaring in our wake, and I suddenly had flashbacks of New York City.

We stopped when we came to a park.

As we caught our breath near a playground, Tunde, Teo, Stella, and Javiera caught up with us. We were all sweating and delirious, none of us having had more than a few hours' sleep on the flight over. The adrenaline that had been driving me ebbed, and my limbs felt as heavy as stone pillars.

"We need to get in there," I said, "but . . ."

"But what?" Tunde asked.

"It's going to be a nightmare, and time is ticking down fast."

Tunde nodded. "I am afraid this truly is the best of the brain trust. These people are working inside a fortress; all of the hardware is excessive. Even if we could sneak inside and bring in more advanced cameras or microphones, it is very unlikely we would not be seen or even that our signal would make it out."

We all thought on that a moment, racking our brains.

"So we can't get in . . . ," I said, letting out a sigh of frustration.

"And Kiran will engage the virus tomorrow," Cai added.

Great. Rex, if you've got some secret weapon, now's the time to use it.

We needed a place to go—a place to lie low and think.

Truth is: This wasn't going to be like Kolkata or Beijing.

Then, they had no idea we were coming. The Mexico City black box lab presented a formidable challenge—maybe the biggest we'd faced yet.

There was, in my mind, only one place to go.

Home.

14.5

We took two cabs across town to an apartment building just off Plaza Carso.

Plaza Carso

After we'd piled out of the vehicles and tipped the drivers, we stood across the street from the building and I pointed to a window on the top floor.

"You remember?" I asked Teo.

"Yeah," he said. "This is going to be really tough."

We were standing across the street from my aunt and uncle's apartment. This was my father's brother, Ernesto. He was older than Papa by three years and worked as a pharmacist in a drugstore downtown. Ernesto was married to Josefa, a nurse. They'd raised two kids, both now off to college, and had an apartment filled with potted plants and fish tanks.

Despite my question to Teo, he and I had never been to Mexico.

But we knew this place; we knew it from photographs that filled the albums on the bookshelf on Ma and Papa's room. We'd studied those photos so carefully, so intently, over the years that we could practically smell the earthy scent of the apartment. Even though I'd never stepped foot in it, I knew every room by heart.

When Teo said this was going to be tough, he wasn't talking about climbing the four floors to my aunt and uncle's place.

He was talking about coming clean.

About seeing Ma and Papa for the first time since he'd vanished.

Teo was sweating while we climbed the apartment steps. Tunde was right behind me, eager and excited as ever. The guy's energy never seemed to flag. Cai was at the back of the line with Ivan. As we walked, they talked game theory.

I took a moment at the door.

My aunt and uncle, Ma and Papa, they had no idea we were going to be stopping by. They certainly had no idea that

they'd be seeing Teo. I decided it'd be better if I was the one to knock, the first face they saw.

"You ready?" I asked Teo as he stood behind me.

"No," he said.

"Sorry, man. World's hanging in the balance here."

I knocked on the door three times. My uncle Ernesto answered, his cheeks red with laughter, and his eyes went instantly wide. He stepped backward, confused, not saying a word as my aunt called to him from the other room.

"Who is at the door?" she asked in Spanish.

"Rex . . . ," Ernesto said, stunned. "And a bunch of other people . . ."

Within seconds, Ma, Papa, and Aunt Josefa were standing behind him. For a split second there was this monumental silence. All of us—me, Teo, the LODGE, ULTRA, my family—staring at each other, caught up in this singular instant of incredible emotion. And then the dam broke. Ma burst into tears as she took Teo in her arms. Teo cried rivers. And I cried as well.

It felt like hours before we actually stepped inside.

After the tears, we sat in the living room, Teo on a couch with Ma and Papa; Tunde and Stella in chairs alongside my aunt and uncle; and Cai, Ivan, Javiera, and me on pillows on the floor. Teo opened up—I don't know if it was the weight lifted from his shoulders after the Terminal takedown or that, finally, he was home—and told us everything he'd been up to. He didn't get into the specifics of his research, but he told us about the places he'd visited, the adventures he'd had.

The night he vanished, he caught a ride with a Terminal associate—someone like him, eager to make a difference but not fully convinced the hacktivist group really could accomplish what they'd set out to do. First stop was Houston. Then they traveled to Europe—Zurich for a few months, living in a loft, then to Cyprus.

The first problems began there—Teo had become aware of Kiran's work as OndScan grew bigger and bigger. He knew, even back then, two years ago, that Kiran was a threat. He couldn't convince Terminal, so he broke ranks.

Still, he didn't quit completely.

Just kept finding himself drawn to their radical way of doing things. He reached out to Terminal from the shadows—well, really just the encrypted dark Web—and ran innocuous side missions. One-offs that made him feel as though he was making a difference while he toiled away in secret. Wasn't exactly the life he'd run away from home for, but he settled into it.

He moved to New York.

Got his apartment.

Teo did what he could on his own. Working on the bio-computer, attempting to come up with a secure method of storing and moving data organically. The idea was to come up with something neither Kiran nor Terminal could access.

His was a life of leftovers, biochemistry, and loneliness.

This went on for a long time.

And then the Game happened, I reappeared, WALKABOUT went online, and Kiran came after me. With the LODGE on the run, Teo decided it was time to reach out. He left clues where he could, led us to the lab, and followed Kiran to India. My joining Kiran there, though not intended, was like a puzzle coming together.

Crazily enough, he actually thought he might be able to

convince me to join Terminal, that the two of us could utilize their techniques and make their mission a success without all the chaos and negativity. Obviously, that didn't work out.

After getting it all off his chest, Teo settled back into the couch.

He put his arms around Ma and Papa.

As he'd told his story, I'd watched their faces as they moved through shock and then worry to acceptance and happiness. It was an emotional roller coaster that they wore on their faces. Seeing them all sitting together was an image I'd longed to see for years. Finally witnessing it, I almost had no words to describe my joy.

Papa said, "It is wonderful to have you home again, son."

To which Ma added: "But never, never again can you put us through that."

Teo nodded, understanding. "I promise, I won't."

Life was suddenly good again.

Only it wasn't.

The LODGE and ULTRA had some serious work to do. While Ma and Papa went up to the roof to get some evening air and talk more, we talked shop.

"So we know we can't do what we've done before," I said.

"Well," Tunde began, "Stella and I could build a machine that could get inside. With the two of us, it would go much faster—"

"No time," Cai said. "Besides, they'll be looking for us to try to get in."

"Don't have time to hack our way in, either," Javiera said.

We sat in silence for a few moments, stuck.

Ivan suggested something with projections, Javiera came

155

up with an idea to hack into their systems further up the "digital line," and I threw out an admittedly wacky idea involving mirrors. But none of them got us anywhere.

We'd hit a dead end.

Suddenly, Tunde stood up. "We need tacos," he said.

"Hang on," Stella spoke for all of us, "what?"

"Tacos." Tunde beamed.

15. TUNDE

My friends, the best way to break through a logjam of thought is to eat!

I am not kidding in the least. Oftentimes, when I am stuck with a problem that cannot be solved by any normal means, I find that distracting my poor, overloaded brain with food is essential. I do not know the chemistry of how nutrients impact the brain cells, but I am certain that the right combination of minerals is crucial to improved mental flow.

I knew that tacos could only help.

Na today I dey realized dis truth.

We were in Mexico City after all!

It was, however, quite late in the evening. Though some of them put up more of a fuss than others, everyone agreed with me that getting out into the night air would be ideal. Mrs. Huerta, the aunt, suggested we try a taco stand on the corner just a block from the apartment. She insisted it was the finest taco stand in the whole of the country. This, of course, made me only the hungrier!

We all piled out into the street.

Ah, *omos*, the air was filled with the intoxicating smell of tropical flowers and the earthy scent of recent rain. The streets were wet and reflected the dizzying lights that flickered and flashed above us. I was in love with this city already.

We found the taco stand, and, thrillingly, it was still serving tacos. My friends, these little bites of heaven were incredible! I had heard about tacos before, likely from a television program or on the Internet, but those were in hard shells and looked a little too . . . organized. These tacos were gently laid out on little pancakes of flour. The ones that I ate contained braised pork, beans, cheese, avocado leaves, and a strange mushroom-like thing that Rex told me was corn fungus. My friends, I devoured five of the delicious things before the idea struck me.

It was not so much a bolt out of the blue as it was a sudden realization that the answer to our dilemma was right in front of my face. The taco was what inspired me. As I ate it, the shell worked quite hard to keep its contents contained but eventually failed. All of the wonderful filling poured out into my hands. Rather than the mess annoying me, it gave me an incredible idea.

"I have it!" I shouted to my friends in the LODGE and ULTRA.

"Have what?" Rex asked, nearly choking on his food.

"How we are going to get into that black box lab!"

I gathered everyone around. "We cannot get into this facility," I said. "We cannot break in physically or digitally. We also do not have the time to plot or build. So, the only answer is to not get inside."

"That's really deep, Tunde," my best friend said.

"We are not going in," I repeated. "They are coming out."

"The brain trust?" Ivan asked, flabbergasted.

"Yes," I said. "And they will bring their data with them."

Rex looked at me as though I was crazy.

But I dey not craise, oh!

"My friend," I said, "we all came outside into the night to get these delicious tacos because we knew that we needed them. We are going to convince the brain trust prodigies in that lab to come outside because they need to as well."

"So we scare them out?" Stella asked. "Start a fire or—"

"No." I shook my head. "No, nothing so crude. *Sorry.*"

"Okay . . . ," Javiera said, looking at me quizzically. "Then how?"

"That is the most beautiful part," I continued. "We are going to show them the error of their ways. We will show them what we know, give them our information. Reveal to them the truth of what Kiran is doing and what those programs they are working on will do to the world. Once they see the truth of it, they will stop."

"Seems awfully optimistic," Ivan said.

I took my final bites of taco and said, "There are very few truly evil people, Ivan. I believe that the brain trust members are like those friends of Terminal who thought they were changing the world and just did not see the destructive side of what they were doing. Perhaps there are some bad brain trusters, though again I do not like that word. My guess is that even so, they are few in number. If we can convince the majority to rebel, they will."

"Don't you think they already know what Kiran's doing?" Javiera asked. "I mean they're working on these projects twenty-four-seven."

"I think they see what they want to see. We will change the want."

"Now you're getting philosophical," Rex said.

Cai jumped in next. "Say we can convince them, and say we've got the information that will do that. How do you suggest we get this data to them? We've already decided that hacking our way in won't work."

"We will not hack," I said. "We will share."

This response got me even more confused looks, but I had a plan—a very clever, very crazy plan.

15.1

48 HOURS UNTIL SHIVA

"We are going to use crowds," I said.

I explained my idea to Cai and Ivan and was enthused that they agreed it was a good idea. We could not hack directly into the Mexico City black box lab, this much was clear from Rex and Javiera, but we could influence the influencers inside. I left how that would happen to Cai.

"If we can crowdsource the messaging," Cai said, "we can get people, all of our followers, ULTRA's followers, to communicate privately with the brain trust people inside the lab. Once we get their attention, we can direct them to some sort of data feed. Something independent of Kiran's closed system."

"Independent how?" Rex asked.

"What we need," Ivan said, "is a way to envelop the entire building and all of its communication systems in a single, wireless network. Basically, we need to make a digital bubble around them and control what goes into that bubble."

"Leave that to Stella and me," I said, looking to Stella.

With our brains already racing, we rushed back to the

apartment and caught Teo up on the details of our plan. Though many of those details were still left undecided, Teo seemed quite eager to begin immediately. And that is how, my friends, the apartment quickly transformed into a working station.

The parents of my best friend were delighted to find their sons working in tandem again. I myself was cheered to see it. For the first time since I had known him, Rex appeared to be confidently optimistic. I do not know if my own mental outlook had now fully rubbed off on him, but it was excellent to see. It made all of us that much more motivated!

Even though I am not a midnight candle burner, I was delighted to find that Mexico City never slept. Using money loaned to us by the Huertas, we were able to acquire the majority of the things we would need to put our plan in action. By dawn, Stella and I had not only designed one of the most striking and original wireless network systems ever invented but we had most of the parts assembled.

Though it sounds silly, we needed a lot of helium.

Here is the crazy plan we concocted: The only way to create a wireless network that would envelop the Mexico City black box lab was to literally blanket the building with a signal. This signal would both act as a transmission, sending information inside, while at the same time blocking external data from entering. This was the bubble that Ivan envisioned. But how could we create such a thing? Well, we certainly could not rewire the building. We needed a fast and cheap alternative. This meant suspending thousands of tiny transmitters around and over the Mexico City black box lab. My friends, the idea I had was as playful as it was expeditious: We would float hundreds of helium-filled balloons over the site!

The trick, of course, would be to ensure that the balloons did not drift over the city and then up into the sky. Not only would we need to tether them, but we would have to calibrate the precise weight for each to hover properly over the rooftop building and keep the dome shape we would need. When all the transmitters held aloft were activated, they would create a bubble network around the Mexico City black box lab and we would be in total control of it!

Stella and I worked out the details of the transmitters. Luckily, these would not be items we had to fabricate, since creating thousands of them by hand within the allotted time would be impossible. We would use existing pieces, tiny single-chip transmitters that were a quarter the size of a penny coin, that were easily found in cast-off computer parts. We could harvest most of them from older cell phones.

At the same time, Rex and Javiera set about the complicated task of programming them, and Teo, Cai, and Ivan determined what information we would share with the brain trust. It had to be both convincing and straightforward; we certainly could not afford for the people inside the lab to sit around and debate the ideas they were receiving.

I am happy to say that Stella and I got along quite well. Though we were not always in sync—we had several fierce debates about the proper power supply to use—she and I came from the same mindset about recycling.

We both loved dumps!

It took us until dawn to finish the balloon transmitter array. By the time the hardware was built, programmed, and readied, we had four hundred balloons filled with helium under a tarp on the apartment rooftop. It was quite a colorful sight, like a nest of churning rainbows. Mr. and Mrs. Huerta, along with the aunt and uncle, came out with coffee and sweet rolls a few minutes after we had finished our work. They were stunned to see all the balloons.

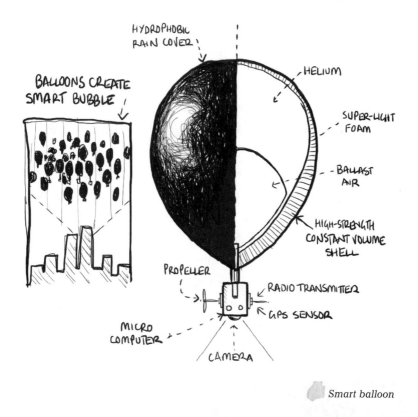

Smart balloon

"This is . . . ," Mr. Huerta began but paused. "This is wild."

"Wait until you see it in action," I said. "We are going to make quite a scene."

15.2

In Naija-land we have a saying, "A frog does not jump in the daytime without reason."

You may consider this a silly proverb, but the truth of it is quite profound. A frog does not have many defenses. It must use stealth and, often, the cover of darkness to travel about and do frog-like things. So a frog moving about in the daylight is surely a risk-taking frog. The reasons for its being out must be very, very important. Or we are talking about a seriously crazy frog.

Regardless, this is the same approach that the LODGE and ULTRA took.

Rather than attempting to surreptitiously plant the balloon array around the Mexico City black box lab, we marched down the street with our giant bags of balloons. It was still early in the morning, not yet seven a.m., but we wanted to make a spectacle. It was, of course, an idea that Cai had.

"If we sneak around," she said as we readied all our equipment, "people will become suspicious and call the police quickly. If we walk down the sidewalk like revelers headed to a party, people will assume that is exactly what we are. We can say something about this being the grand opening of the black box lab."

We all laughed at that, though Cai insisted it was somewhat true.

Mr. and Mrs. Huerta transported us, and our equipment, in a rental van to a spot two blocks from the black box lab. The balloons themselves were under a clear tarp strapped gently to the roof of the van. It was quite a sight.

Once we arrived, we began our spectacle.

Being myself, I did worry about accidentally causing car crashes due to the fact that we might be distracting drivers. But this worry came to naught; there was quite a traffic jam along our route and, if anything, we cheered those anxious commuters!

"What are we showing them?" I asked Cai as we walked.

"It was tricky coming up with the most effective material," she said. "These are people like us, prodigies looking for ways to use their gifts to better the world. They've bought into Kiran's concepts, his whole song and dance. We realized it would be too hard to get them to completely dismiss Kiran himself—"

"Why is that?" I asked. "He does many bad things."

"But he does them out of a twisted belief that they lead to good things."

"Ah," I said, "I see. So, if you cannot make him look bad . . ."

"Then we make what he does look bad," Cai continued. "We need them to see the end result of his actions. If we can show them what that virus they're about to release is going to do—if we can show them how bad Shiva will be—then we can convince them that they don't want to be part of it. They don't necessarily have to hate Kiran, but they need to see him as misguided."

"That way they still feel good about themselves."

"Right," Cai said. "We don't want them to feel like monsters for working on this project with OndScan. Guilt will just poison them more. We want these people to be on our side, to join us."

Ah, Cai, always the wisest!

Once we got to the black box lab, we put our plan in motion. While Rex, Teo, and Javiera went to the roof of the neighboring building that housed all of the satellite dishes and radio antennae to begin the broadcast, Stella and I began releasing the balloons around the exterior of the lab. The trick was spacing them properly: too far apart and the signals would weaken; too close and they would overlap and, also, weaken. We tethered them all around five feet apart. By the time we had finished putting the balloons up fifty-three minutes later, it gave the Mexico City black box lab the feel of a carnival. So many colors!

With the balloons in place, I gave the signal to Rex.

Though it was silent, when he flicked on the network, Stella and I were able to view the feed through our cell phones. We sat side by side on the edge of the lab roof and watched as it all unfolded just beneath us.

Cai and Ivan had certainly outdone themselves.

The very first thing that happened was that every connected screen inside the lab flashed three times, an excellent way to get attention, before cutting to a shot of Cai done up in her finest Painted Wolf makeup and clothing. Her face filled most of the frame, and even though she was wearing her trademark sunglasses, you could feel her eyes burning straight into your cerebral cortex.

"Kiran has been lying to you," she said in English. "The virus you are preparing will not usher in a new age of equality. Shiva will instead cause senseless and useless destruction, destruction that you will be a part of. Watch. . . ."

What followed was a cavalcade of imagery and documents, all from the files we had accumulated after Rex made his way into the Kolkata lab, the codes we had acquired in Beijing, the work Teo had done while in hiding, and the reams of things ULTRA had gathered up over the past few weeks. One did not need to have a degree in coding or advanced mathematics to see the overall effect. Pulling all of these disparate pieces together and revealing the overall shape of the puzzle was enough. The truth was simple: The brain trusters inside the Mexico City black box lab had never actually seen the full extent of what they were working on. They were like factory workers who only make a part of an apparatus but never see the full scope of the machine. We needed to show them what they were actually doing.

After the images and papers, the codes and secret e-mails, flickered across the screen, Cai reappeared. I am not ashamed to tell you that much to the bemusement of Stella, I clapped and cheered.

Painted Wolf said, "Now that you've seen what you've spent the past few weeks creating, you have a choice: You can attempt to help Kiran bring destruction to the world or you can join us and create real change. Brain trust, step outside of your lab, walk out into the street. We are waiting. Join us."

The screen flashed again and then went to black.

I turned to Stella. She was grinning ear to ear.

45 HOURS UNTIL SHIVA

It took two minutes for the first of the brain trust members to emerge.

The metal door to the black box lab slid open, and a teenaged boy stepped out, blinking in the early morning light. He was lanky like Rex and had his hair in an Afro. I was standing there, alongside Ivan, with a simple paper sign that read:

WELCOME TO THE REVOLUTION.

The teenaged boy walked over to me and said, "My name is Alfonso."

"Hi, Alfonso. I'm Painted Wolf."

"I, uh, I designed a lot of the infection mechanism the virus uses," Alfonso said, a bit nervous. "I want to help you. I want to make things right."

"Excellent," I said. "Thank you. What stage is Shiva at now?"

Alfonso looked a bit surprised that I'd mentioned Kiran's program by name, but he didn't let it stop him for long. He said, "The program is up and running."

"Do you have any way to access it?"

"No," he said. "The way the program's designed, once it's finalized, Kiran takes full control of it. He's the one who pulls the trigger, so to speak."

"And there are no back channels? No remnant access codes?" Rex asked.

Alfonso shook his head. "Kiran wanted it bulletproof."

"He knew we would be trying," Tunde said, walking over to the conversation. "Kiran is no dummy. He and General Iyabo share the same trait for ultimate control. My worry is that the only way to truly stop the Shiva program is to take it from Kiran ourselves."

"Can you tell us what Shiva will do?" Rex asked Alfonso. "I think we have a cursory idea of how it will hit banking accounts, businesses, and governments, but is there more beyond that?"

Alfonso sighed, long and loud.

"It'll delete everything on the Internet," he said.

We all looked at each other. As Rex had said, we all had a general idea of what exactly Shiva might accomplish, but I don't think we truly realized the extent. To hear it so plainly made it sound that much worse.

Alfonso could read our worry. He said, "But while we don't have the key to stop Shiva, there is something we do have."

He turned and signaled to a girl with a metal briefcase.

"This is what you're looking for," the girl told me.

"What is this?" I asked as she handed me a briefcase.

"This is Rama," Alfonso said. "Take a look."

He opened the briefcase and revealed its contents. Inside was a single sheet of shiny metal the size of a standard index card, roughly three by five inches. The "metal paper" was as thin as regular paper but marked by various engraved dots and swirls, almost like the perforations on a sheet of stamps.

Rex stepped up alongside me and examined the paper.

"This what I think it is?"

Alfonso nodded. "Shiva was a virus, a program designed to wipe the slate clean," he said. "And Rama is supposed to be the next step, a new Internet, a new world of data. Sizewise, Rama is twenty times bigger than Shiva. The trick was storing all that data in a way that could be easily transported. We chose to store it on state-of-the-art, nonvolatile, solid-state memory sheets. These involve memristors and allow us to make the storage devices quite small. This card, in fact, holds nearly a quarter of the Rama program."

"Incredible," I said. "And how do we **extract the data**?"

The brain trust girl said, "These."

She pulled a scanner from her back pocket. The size of a cell phone, it resembled a magnifying glass, only the glass part was not clear but dark. She said, "This is positioned above the sheet—there is a stand inside each briefcase—and when it's switched on, it will scan the data and transcribe it to whatever device you have linked up. Probably best to set it up with a laptop or a tablet computer."

"And how long does that take?" I asked.

"Twenty minutes a sheet, give or take," she said.

"How many sheets?" Rex asked.

"Ten," Alfonso said.

I turned to see an additional nine brain trusters emerging with briefcases. We had the Rama code, the second part of Kiran's grand plan.

Within the next fifteen minutes, all of the brain trusters walked out of the lab and into the street. There were forty of them all together. They stood around, talking to each of us, telling us what their area of expertise was and how they wanted to help. Even better, a good number of them came out of the black box lab holding flash drives, binders, and even laptops.

Our plan had worked.

And just in time, too. As we stood there conversing, several of the helium balloons holding network transmitters popped overhead. The balloons sank, their contents falling to the street. The network was disabled and our **signal lost.**

Watching Tunde and Rex talk to the brain trusters was incredibly inspiring. I'd never considered the brain trust people to be enemies, just deluded kids who wanted to do the best thing for the world but found the wrong route. We'd taken down Terminal, and now we'd liberated the brain trust. Two threats were disabled, but we weren't close to done.

Kiran still had Shiva in hand.

16.1

Though Kiran had lost most, if not all, of his brain trust, I knew he was still dangerous.

One of the established concepts in game theory is unpredictability. Though it sounds like a contradiction, being unpredictable is a rational strategy. When you and your opponent have clashing ideologies, game theory says that you should behave in a way that leaves your opponent figuring out your intentions. If you move randomly, it's difficult for them to outguess you.

We'd been outguessing Kiran for a few moves, but I knew he always retained the upper hand. Even with Rama, we still didn't know what Kiran's next move would be. My guess was that he'd **launch Shiva**. Even without Rama as the backup, he'd still get what he wanted: an overturn of the status quo.

Our next step had to be tracking him down.

Working with ULTRA and the brain trust, we moved all of the records, documents, and digital drives to Rex's aunt and uncle's apartment. I felt really bad knocking on their door that afternoon. Rex's uncle Ernesto's eyes bugged out when he saw we had a dozen more people with us than the day before. Luckily, the weather was good and the roof was large. We spread everything we could out on the hard-top, put up deck umbrellas, and settled in to go over what we'd acquired.

As the sun set, I decided I needed a break. I walked over to the water tower on the roof and sat on one of the steps that led up to it. The tower was squat like a gourd, and someone had painted it bright blue with a giant smiley face. It stared out over Mexico City with an eternal grin, no matter the weather or what took place below. I sat there a few moments, collecting my thoughts and noticing a scratch I'd somehow gotten on the back of my left hand, before Rex sat down beside me with a glass of water and a snack.

"So what brings you to Mexico?" he joked.

Then he took my hand and ran his fingers over it, noticing the cut.

"You need a bandage or something?"

It was a silly question; the cut was small.

"It's nothing."

"Looks like it hurt."

"It's a scratch," I said. "I can handle a scratch."

"I'm sure you can. You look **pretty tough.**"

"You flirting with me, Mr. Huerta?"

Rex winked.

For a second, I imagined us out on an actual, real-life date, but I couldn't really see what that would look like. Definitely not us.

We both started laughing.

Then, as our chuckles ebbed, Rex got serious.

"The Rama program is something," Rex said, "that I haven't really dug into as deeply as I want to, but it's impressive. If Kiran didn't have the whole Shiva destruction thing, I could see Rama actually being a real gift to the world."

"Think we can reprogram it?"

Rex nodded. "It'll take time, but even if we strip it down to its parts, those are going to be some seriously helpful bits of code."

We sat in silence for a moment. Enjoying each other's company and looking out as the sun's last few orange rays painted the horizon.

"Kiran's going to fight with everything he's got," I said.

"And we're stronger now than we've ever been."

"You really think so?"

"I know so," Rex said.

Tunde shouted from across the rooftop, "Here!"

Rex and I hopped down from the water tank's steps and raced over to where Tunde was sitting. He was on a blanket under an umbrella going over several laptop computers with Stella, Javiera, and a couple of the brain trusters.

"What'd you find?" I asked Tunde as I sat down beside him.

"A location," Tunde said.

He turned a laptop around and handed it to me. On the screen was a map of the United States, but it didn't look like the sort of map I was familiar with. This one was blue with a lot of rings radiating from a million little points. Tunde pointed to one of the points in the south of the country.

"There," he said. "That is Kiran."

"That's where he is?" I asked, feeling my adrenaline surge again.

"No," Tunde said. "It is actually just one ping on a cellular tower. He is somewhere near there, and if we can find additional pings, we can triangulate his location from them. My ULTRA and brain trust friends here have performed some amazing feats of digital wizardry, and I have no doubt they will be able to locate Kiran in the next few hours. But it will not be faster than that."

"That's excellent, Tunde," I said, smiling to everyone.

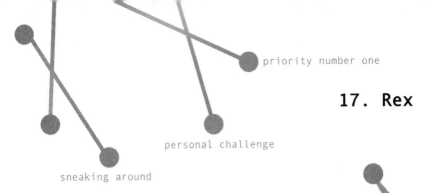

priority number one

sneaking around

personal challenge

17. Rex

43.5 HOURS UNTIL SHIVA

Stopping Kiran was obviously priority number one, but Teo and I had another problem we had to solve.

I was pretty much confident that with the combined brain power of the LODGE, ULTRA, and the kids from the brain trust, we'd be able to pinpoint Kiran's location. Heck, we'd already done several impossible things before dinner.

Getting my parents back to the States, however, was a more personal challenge.

While everyone worked on the stuff we'd snagged from the black box lab, I pulled my brother aside for a conversation. This new version of my brother, the guy who seemed adept at sneaking around borders and trotting the globe untracked, needed to show me how we were going to get our family back to Santa Cruz.

We decided to make a coffee run.

"There's a great café three blocks from here," Teo said.

After we'd collected everyone's orders (Tunde insisted on tea instead of coffee, of course), we walked downstairs and out into the city. The place was full of music and life: people in bright colors having incredibly animated conversations and the sound of percussion drifting out of every storefront.

"It's not going to be as hard as you think," Teo said.

Like I'd believe that.

"Go on," I replied.

"Remember my first year of college? Biochem?"

"The class you made up a fake identity to attend?"

"Right."

True story: Teo was in his first year at college and desperately wanted to be in this one advanced biochemistry class. But the school insisted that you couldn't just skip courses, no matter how smart you were. So he made up this avatar, this fake Teo named Toro, gave himself all the requisite credits, and attended the class. The school, crazily, never caught on.

"What about it?" I asked.

"That's how we're getting Ma and Papa back home and . . ."

Teo stopped on a corner, and that's when I realized we were standing across the street from where we'd been that morning—Kiran's Mexico City black box lab. We'd come from a different direction, and I was a bit turned around.

". . . this is how we do it," Teo finished.

"Doesn't look like a café," I said.

"The kids from Kiran's team, the brain trust, they told me there's a supercomputer inside the building. It's not quantum, but most of those have been pretty much effectively locked down since Kiran got ahold of WALKABOUT. You're the king on the specs, but they told me the machine's fast. Very fast. One point nine petaflop performance speeds, forty thousand six-core processors."

Fast indeed, but . . .

"Okay," I said. "Now's the part where you try to convince

me we actually need to use a superfast supercomputer. What're you thinking?"

"Kiran ghosted you and your friends; we can ghost our parents."

"To do that we'd need the same access to WALKABOUT Kiran has."

Teo smiled. "You put in a back door, remember? India was just a few days ago, Rex. I'm starting to worry about you."

I hadn't forgotten about the tweaks I'd pulled on WALKABOUT 2.0 in Kolkata, but I'd always intended them as a way to backstab Kiran. Leave it to my older, more devious, brother to use the back door to fool the authorities and sneak our parents back into the United States. Thing is, we were on our way to coffee, not a break-in.

"You're not actually thinking of doing this now. . . ."

Teo nodded. "Of course, brother. When else would we do it?"

17.1

"Everything we'll need is inside," Teo said.

"Sounds too easy."

"It is."

The way I saw it, we had maybe twenty minutes.

Of course, I would have gladly spent every waking moment trying to get our parents home. But I knew we were on a tight schedule. A countdown to Armageddon we couldn't ignore. It was time to push ourselves.

Twenty minutes it is. We crossed the intersection to the front door of the black box lab. Teo paused before the biometric lock. "I've hacked these things before," he said. "Can usually get into one within three, four minutes. I'm not worried about the lock on this door. But if I open it, it's going to trigger some security measures on the network inside. The whole balloon thing established a bubble network, but the system still running inside here is all Kiran."

"So you're saying the minute we step into this place it'll set off alarms and Kiran's going to know we're in here."

Teo nodded as he began hacking the lock.

"So," I continued, "basically, we step into this building right now and it'll put into jeopardy everything the LODGE and ULTRA have worked toward for the past forty-eight hours. We'll be tipping off Kiran."

Teo said, "You got it. It's also going to shorten our time inside."

"Like what?"

"Like we'll maybe have ten minutes."

So much for twenty . . .

I mentally played out our time inside the black box lab. We'd have to move fast, disable whatever cameras and alarms we found, tap into the network, take out Kiran's security software, hit the supercomputer, get into the necessary government networks, change data, cover our tracks, and then get out of the building in as little time as possible and pray the whole run back to our aunt and uncle's apartment.

Easy, right? But . . .

The stakes were huge. If Cai had been there, she would have had us debating the merits and mistakes of such a decision. I'd learned enough from her to better gauge risk. She took risks all the time, but they were smart risks. This, this seemed pretty damn dumb. And yet, it was my parents.

They need to be home, Rex. This is all your fault.

"We go in here," I said. "And I need you to do everything

alarms

cameras

supercomputer

I say, when I say it. We can't mess around, brother. I need you to trust me on this."

Teo nodded his acknowledgment and placed his hand on the scanner.

The door unlocked with a clank, and we were inside. The lights flickered on automatically as we walked across the main room. The black box lab felt entirely different deserted. As expected, alarms went off. Lights flashed. The whole place felt like it was going to explode in a matter of minutes. I snatched a laser pointer off a desk near an electronic whiteboard and took out the few ceiling cameras I saw.

"There," I said, pointing to a back staircase.

I had to yell over the blaring alarms.

We ran over to the stairs and barreled down them fast as possible.

Sure enough, there was a supercomputer that filled the entire basement. It was massive, long lines of servers housed in black rectangular boxes that gave the thing a sort of ominous look. There was a logo of an angry, fanged cobra printed on the side of each server housing; above each serpent was the word *Naga*.

"Naga," Teo said. "The great snake of Hindu mythology."

"Doesn't look like a nice guy."

"He causes earthquakes," Teo said.

That gave me little comfort as I settled into a rolling chair at the access terminal for Naga. It felt like I was sitting behind the wheel of a bullet train. Just a single monitor and keyboard to control this monster of a machine. Teo dragged another rolling chair over and sat beside me.

Thankfully the scream of the alarms was quieter in the basement.

I looked at my watch; five minutes had passed.

"You can do this, Rex," Teo said. "Just focus."

Getting past the log-in screen was relatively easy. Even though the password was automatically updated every three minutes, I was able to brute force hack my way past it. Once I was in the system, however, all the security software kicked into gear, hitting me at every turn. That sounds like a video game—but it's really not. Hacking is numbers and code and zero graphics.

The excitement, it happens in your head.

I spent an additional two minutes getting past the security systems. I'll admit: I should have been faster, but the system was pretty complex and it took me a while to find what I needed. Some less organized brain trust member had forgotten to update a few programs. They were minor, nothing directly related to the security system, but when I accessed and tweaked them, they caused a cascade of failures. I used those to burrow my way fully into the system. Score one for Rex.

Now that I had control of Naga, it was only a matter of tracking down WALKABOUT 2.0 and getting it up and running. That was the most dangerous move I'd make, the one that would be sure to alert Kiran.

Sure enough, WALKABOUT 2.0 was loaded onto the supercomputer.

Before I opened the program, I hesitated.

Teo noticed.

"You have a back door," he said. "What's the problem?"

"Kiran might have discovered it."

"Wouldn't you know?"

"Kiran's smarter than the average coder," I said. "He'd

leave it open. He'd wait for me to access it and then spring whatever trap he has planned. Then again, maybe he hasn't even discovered it. Maybe he's been too busy protecting his interests."

"Odds he found it?" Teo asked.

I thought a second, finger hovering over the enter button.

"Sixty, sixty-five percent," I said.

Teo put his hand on my shoulder. "We've come this far."

We'd already broken in, taken control of Naga; if Kiran wasn't already aware we were in his system then he was in a coma or something. And if he knew that I was hacking Naga, he knew I'd be going for WALKABOUT 2.0. There was no other choice: I had to access the back door program and run it fast as possible.

"Here goes everything," I said, hitting the enter button.

WALKABOUT 2.0 opened and nothing happened. I searched for Ma and Papa's information, accessing their files and quickly altering them. I cleared the arrest and deportation orders, expunged the records of every note related to their expulsion from the country.

Watching, Teo said, "Make them citizens."

Of course, I'd thought about that. I'd considered it the minute we entered the building, but I knew it'd be the wrong thing to do. Even what I had done, the wiping out of their records, pushed the ethical limits to near-breaking point. My parents had been deported on account of my failings, but it didn't excuse the fact that they'd sneaked into the United States illegally. I couldn't do it.

"No, Teo," I said. "We're doing this the right way."

Parents effectively ghosted, I made my way out of WALKABOUT 2.0.

But I didn't go quietly.

"I'm sure Kiran knows we're here," I said. "He's expecting me to access WALKABOUT 2.0, but he's not going to anticipate this."

What happened next was an on-the-fly decision. It came from the deepest part of my being, a powerful mix of intellect and emotion. I felt like I was in this crazy, Zen state where time seemed to slow to a crawl and I could see the outcome of my decision a dozen years off. And it was a good one; it was the right thing to do.

I logged in to a site I'd created a few years earlier. One I hadn't touched since the Game began. It was a zoo of sorts, a place where I collected and took apart computer viruses, Trojans, and worms; a site to cannibalize them and take the coolest bits of code to use in my other programs.

I selected a particularly noxious worm called DrummB.

This little monster deleted program files wherever it found them and was particularly difficult to remove. Within seconds it could disable WALKABOUT 2.0, and given a couple minutes, it would effectively destroy it.

I downloaded DrummB and launched it.

WALKABOUT 2.0, the "upgraded" version of a program I'd spent two years of my life perfecting to find Teo, the program I'd spilled most of my brain into, was now effectively dead. Destroyed. Erased from history. I'm not going to lie: It felt like I'd just been punched in the gut. Watching WALKABOUT be dismantled, I couldn't help but recall the desperate hours I'd spent creating it. All those delirious coding sessions had worked—Teo was essentially home—but it still hurt to watch.

Two years of work took forty-seven seconds to vanish.

And then I introduced DrummB to Naga itself.

Teo tried to stop me. "What're you doing? We could use it!"

"I can't leave a weapon like this lying around," I said. "It ends here."

As DrummB ate its way through Naga's programs, Teo and I ran back upstairs, through the empty halls of the Mexico City black box lab, and then out into the streets. It was raining, and lightning cut up the sky.

18. TUNDE

42.5 HOURS UNTIL SHIVA

Despite the fact that it was raining and I had been on my feet and jittery from adrenaline for nearly two days straight, I had incredible fun with the brain trust.

While I had been skeptical about the prodigies who chose to work with Kiran, just as I had been very reticent to trust Teo initially, I came to discover that they were good people. Misguided maybe but good at heart. What was even more important, however, was that they were incredibly gifted.

At the Game, I had met and been impressed by the young people that Kiran had chosen to surround himself with. They were ambitious and clever. However, Kiran brought out the worst in them. While they were working in the echo chambers of the black boxes, they did not worry about the possible repercussions of their work.

Ah, but this had changed. Now they were out.

As I walked around, stretching my legs, I listened to their conversations.

"I can't believe you were working on that," one young woman with a nose ring exclaimed to a short boy in a flannel shirt. "I thought I was the only one."

"Insane!" shouted a Thai hydrologist to a Peruvian coder as they transcribed information.

I will not lie to you. I loved to hear these words. It was crazy to know that so many brilliant people worked in the very same rooms and did not understand what their neighbors were truly working on. This, surely, was the worst crime Kiran had perpetrated! To keep all these minds from each other was like separating neurons from one another. Thank goodness we had come along to change it.

But they would have time to do all of this later. Now we needed them to focus on stopping Kiran. On reversing the work that they had already done. Key to succeeding was tracking down Kiran.

E dey hard for us, oh!

Our first order of business was to pull back the curtain.

While each of the brain trust members were busily explaining to the ULTRA team what they had been working on, Cai climbed onto the top of a rather unstable card table we had placed on the rooftop. She called as loudly as she could for each and every person on the roof to listen.

They all turned to her immediately.

"Everyone," she began, "we need to find Kiran."

I saw a lot of heads nodding in understanding.

Cai said, "Working with several of your colleagues, we've identified a rather broad area in Arizona where we think Kiran is currently. To narrow that area down, I need for you to work together. We have to triangulate his location to stop him from proceeding with Shiva."

It did not take long for the brain trust to kick into high gear. Rather than diving into their individual data and work, they began to collaborate, sharing what they knew to try to figure out how we could pinpoint Kiran.

As Cai climbed down from the table, Javiera walked over to us.

"They're empowered now," she said. "They're going to be very helpful."

"That is my sincere hope," I said. "There are some amazing people here."

"Only the best for our friend Kiran."

"Yes, but this is extraordinary," I said. "I have not felt this inspired and impassioned since I was at the Game. Imagine if we could find a way to keep all these beautiful minds together? Find them a home . . ."

"They're not lost puppies, Tunde," Cai said.

"I know this! But just think of the neural power we have congregated on this rooftop. There are about forty-five people up here, and they probably constitute a fifth of the entire prodigy population on the globe. Do you not find it inspiring?"

Javiera looked out over the brain trust members as they talked, typed, and scribbled notes out on scraps of paper. She nodded.

"We should know something by later tonight," Cai said, pleased with their work. "Now, where do you think Rex and Teo have gotten off to?"

"Perhaps they went back to the apartment," I replied. "Let us go there and wait for them. I need to put my feet up, even if it is only for five or six minutes. As they say in my village, my dogs are barking."

"Your dogs?" Cai looked at me sidelong.

"My feet, of course!"

18.1

Rex and Teo came back to the apartment ten minutes after we arrived.

They did not have coffee, or my tea.

Normally, of course, this would not be an incident that would upset me that greatly. I am often quite capable of accomplishing numerous things without the benefit of caffeine. But, my friends, this was simply not one of those times! I expressed my displeasure to Rex.

"*Omo*, what happened?"

"Sorry, Tunde. Something came up," Rex said.

"Something?"

"I will explain in a second. How're we looking up here?"

I proudly gestured back toward the rooftop.

"We have every single member of the brain trust working to triangulate the location in Arizona where Kiran is currently. We will not see the results immediately, of course. But I do believe the tides of war have shifted to our favor."

Rex grabbed my shoulder and gave it a healthy squeeze.

"Excellent, Tunde."

"You said something had come up. What is this something you speak of?"

Rex ignored my question.

"Good, good," Rex said as he placed his arm around my shoulder and began to walk with me toward another part of the rooftop. "Listen, I'm sorry about the tea. Really. I want you to be with me for something important, okay?"

"Yes, of course," I said. I was still a bit confused.

When we reached a quieter corner of the roof, Rex motioned for Cai to join us. She walked over as well, though I could see that Stella and Ivan were a bit perplexed as to why we were having a private discussion without them.

"I kind of did *something*," Rex said.

Cai immediately sensed this "something" was not good.

"What did you do?" I demanded.

"Teo and I went into the Mexico City black box lab," Rex said. "They had a supercomputer in the basement. Not a quantum machine like at the Game but a powerful thing nonetheless. Kiran had WALKABOUT 2.0 loaded on it. I used the program to change my parents' records, to get them back into the States."

I gave my best friend a very serious glance.

"I know," Rex said. "I was desperate. We had to do something. I also destroyed WALKABOUT 2.0. The whole program, every bit of it, is wiped out. Kiran can't use it anymore."

"I do not see why this is so terrible," I said. "You have destroyed a tool that Kiran has used against us in the past. I realize you built it and took great pride in it, but he had corrupted your vision. I am sorry to say this, brother, but I think it is probably a very good thing that the program is destroyed."

"That's not the problem, Tunde," Cai said with her eyes locked on Rex.

"Right," Rex said. "I used the WALKABOUT back door."

"I do not understand the trouble with that . . . ," I said.

"I could have used it to stop Shiva," Rex said, eyeing the floor.

"Should have," Cai said. "It could have easily been accessed."

"I wouldn't say *easily*," Rex countered. "Besides, I don't know if that would have worked. Teo and I didn't exactly have a ton of time in there."

"Well," she said, "now WALKABOUT is gone. Our chance to use it to stop Kiran has evaporated. We're stuck with our original plan, and the clock is ticking. We have to find Kiran in time."

I did not know what to say. To think we may have just lost an opportunity to stop Kiran remotely was almost too much to bear.

By the look of it, Cai was even more furious than me.

"Rex," Cai said, "let's have a talk."

"Fine," he replied. "Just give me a minute."

Rex ushered his parents into the room and told them that he had cleared their records. They were free to return to the United States again. They were shocked and delighted. At the same time, they were deeply concerned that Rex had broken the law.

"But, son," his father said, "what you've done is surely illegal. . . ."

Rex nodded, knowing it was true. "I've broken so many laws during the past few days that it's impossible to even make a list of them. And you and Mama broke the law when you came into the U.S. illegally. But you're good people. You've worked hard to raise Teo and me. Worked hard to make a life for us. I took that away from you, and I wanted to make sure you had it back."

Rex embraced his parents, and, I tell you, my friends, the look upon his face was one of immense contentment. It was truly a joy to see. After all the chaos and worry, Rex had managed to right the wrong he had committed. Though I was still quite angry that he had chosen not to disable Shiva when he had the chance, I will admit that he had made an excellent choice regardless.

"Here's the thing," Rex told his parents. "You don't have much time to pack."

"How much is not much?" Mr. Huerta asked.

"Well," Rex said, "maybe an hour . . . possibly two . . ."

PART THREE

FALL LIKE ROME

38 HOURS UNTIL SHIVA

Rex and I stepped out onto the patio of his aunt and uncle's apartment.

The rain had stopped and the city was gleaming. Though Rex probably thought I was going to yell at him, I wasn't angry so much as disappointed.

"What were you thinking?" I asked Rex.

"I saw an opportunity and I took it."

"And now we have to deal with the fallout," I said. "What if Kiran changes up his plans? What if he **launches Shiva** right now while we're talking? You put everything we'd planned in jeopardy."

"I needed to get my parents home, Cai. The fact that they're here in Mexico City is because of me. I had to fix it."

"You could have done that later. After we'd gotten Kiran."

Rex leaned forward on the railing and sighed.

"I guess I wasn't thinking as clearly as I could have been. I was just so . . . I wanted to get back at him, for stealing my program, for using it to frame the LODGE and me. Since I couldn't hit him in the face, I figured it would feel really good to **hit him where it hurt most,** his empire."

"And did it?"

"For a little bit, yeah," Rex said. "But then reason got hold again."

I stepped over beside him and put a hand on his back.

"So what can we do now?" he asked.

"Keep moving. We can't change our plans. He's likely expecting us to do something completely different now. You changed the board. But I say we stay the course, just exactly as we'd outlined it, and that might trick him. It's like running into a fire. Who would ever do that, right?"

Rex turned from the railing and faced me with a grin.

"You'd run into a fire?" I asked, shaking my head.

"If you were in it, hell yes."

"You're ridiculous," I said. "I'm talking about game theory here, about how to outwit your opponent. I'm saying that maybe we can play this as an opportunity to mix things up. We salvage it by keeping Kiran on his toes."

"So maybe what I did was kind of clever, actually," Rex said.

"Don't you dare . . ."

"Dare what?" Rex feigned shock.

"Turn this around to make it look like you didn't just majorly screw up."

Rex said, "Cai, I admit that I completely and utterly failed. I wasn't thinking; I was just reacting purely on an emotional level. I'm not going to argue it."

Well, that was certainly unexpected.

"Come on," I said. "We need to get to Arizona."

"But we don't even know where Kiran is."

"We're going to have to cross our fingers that the brain trust has located him by the time we touch down. If they haven't, we'll have to do it there. Rex, he's going to take down the entire Internet in a day and a half unless we stop him."

I needed him to understand **the urgency.**

"I get it," he said. "Give me two minutes and I'll have a flight for us."

19.1

36 HOURS UNTIL SHIVA

The flight to Arizona departed two hours later.

We arrived at Aeropuerto Internacional Benito Juárez with just enough time to scramble through security, get onto the plane, and settle into our seats minutes before the jet took off. Tunde and I sat with the ULTRA team in the middle rows of the plane while Rex, Teo, and their parents sat directly behind me.

I wasn't sure what to expect in Arizona, but I planned to use the flight to prepare for our next encounter with Kiran.

As the plane leveled off and the stewards made their way down the aisles with various drinks and snacks for sale, I leaned my seat back, closed my eyes, and walked myself through the various directions our trip could take.

Behind me I could overhear Rex telling his parents about our time in Nigeria. He was describing the feast General Iyabo had prepared for us. As he talked through the tension of that moment, I remembered just how close to being uncovered we were. Recalling just how crazy it all was, I couldn't help but laugh to myself.

Rex's story segued into how he'd found Teo in India. That led to Teo talking about some of his solitary journeys. I couldn't imagine how difficult the past two years had been for

Rex's family. It was amazing sitting there, hearing the reunion continue, as they dove deeper into the emotional toll Teo's running away took on the family. His mother cried again. In fact, they all cried again.

But it was a beautiful thing to hear. There was so much love.

I replayed images of Tunde's village on our departure and saw again how happy his parents and people were to see the general taken away. I recalled our visit to my parents' apartment. How Rex, Teo, and Tunde talked to my father and how I cooked and talked with my mother. Now Rex and Teo were united and their family was again whole for the first time in a very long time.

I only realized I'd fallen asleep when the plane hit turbulence on its descent into Phoenix, Arizona. When I sat up, I noticed that Tunde was fast asleep beside me, his head resting on Stella's shoulder. She was asleep as well.

I took out my cell phone and used an app to hitchhike onto a carrier's signal, allowing me service. There were dozens of messages and texts from Rodger Dodger. She'd heard about our breaking up the brain trust in Mexico City and sent a series of happy face and surprise face emoji. There was also an alert from the brain trust: Kiran was at a house in Phoenix. They sent an aerial map.

Tunde noticed my expression. "You look very pleased," he said.

"We found him," I said.

"What's the plan?" Rex asked.

"We confront him," I said. "Keep him occupied while we bring in the police and do what we can to dismantle Shiva before he launches it."

19.2

We said our good-byes to Rex's parents at Phoenix Sky Harbor International Airport.

They had a plane to Santa Cruz to catch, and we had a car ready to take us to the location the brain trust had sent us. Teo set it up through a friend he trusted. Rex and Teo hugged and kissed their parents, but I could tell they were eager to get back into the chase. Rex in particular, buoyed by the fact that his parents would be home safe soon, seemed especially impatient to get going.

As we exited the airport and made our way to the car, I ran through some of the **strategies** I'd come up with on the flight before I'd fallen asleep. Adapting my plan, considering word that Kiran was on the move, I told everyone the situation.

"This is going to be a house," I said. "In a nice neighborhood."

"So not a black box lab?" Tunde asked.

"No," I replied.

We stepped outside into the bright, dry Arizona air.

Our ride, a van, was waiting on a nearby corner.

As we crossed the street, I continued, "Knowing Kiran, there's a good chance he saw this coming. He's lying low now because even with the superstructure of his grand scheme falling apart, he's still got the trigger for Shiva in his hands. We've turned the brain trust, taken down all his labs, and raided his data, but he's still got the upper hand."

"How is that?" Javiera asked. "Seems we're in control now."

"This is a zero-sum game," I replied. "There is no half winning or half losing. We need to take down all his systems and then crush him as well. I don't like talking in those terms, but it's the truth. As long as Kiran is free, this doesn't end."

"But we already know he's here," Teo said. "I'm confused."

"Kiran has a message for us," I said, "I'm convinced of it. That's been his modus operandi the whole way through. At the Game, he brought me over to his OndScan hangout to see how impressive all his gear was. In India, he showed Rex the inside track with the brain trust and his larger vision. He's doing it again here. Kiran wants us on his team. Wants to show us something that might convince us that he's after the same thing we are."

"And that is . . . ?" Ivan asked.

"A true revolution."

19.3

During the drive to the location, I explained what I meant.

"After everything that's happened, Kiran knows he can't convince us his actions aren't destructive. That cat's pretty much out of the bag now. It's going to be something more along the lines of the puppet master routine he loves to pull. He's probably going to try to convince us he planned all this out, that he already knew what moves we'd make, and that he wanted us to discover his plans so we could prove ourselves."

"He already tried with me," Rex said. "It's flattering."

"Which is exactly what he wants. Whatever we find at this house, don't take it at face value. He knows we're coming for him; whatever we find is going to have been put there on purpose. Hopefully, we can find whatever tiny truths he's scattered through **his gilded lies.** Sorry, that sounded less poetic in my head."

We arrived in the neighborhood ten minutes later.

As it appeared on the aerial shots, it was a nice place with large, expensive homes. Each one had an outdoor pool and perfect landscaping. Many of the houses were hypermodern, looking like odd geometric structures. When we pulled up to the building we'd triangulated, it was massive—a black stone, metal, and glass behemoth with wild, swooping curves. The house honestly looked more like an art museum than a home.

Modernist house

We pulled up to a corner a block away to observe.

There were lights on inside. Within a few seconds of watching the home, we saw movement in an upstairs window. The blinds weren't drawn and the windows were quite large, so it was easy to see inside. Kiran stood at a window and looked out into the darkness as he sipped from a coffee mug.

Teo said, "He's home."

"Think he sees us?" Ivan asked.

"No," I said. I couldn't be sure, but he wasn't looking in our direction. Then again, it was Kiran, so it was hard to say.

"So what do we do now?" Javiera asked.

"We get out of this car, march over there, and confront him," Tunde said.

"And we kick his butt," Stella added.

"That doesn't sound like a very good plan," I said.

Teo said, "Cai's right."

"We need to keep him there, distract him with something. Then, while he's talking like he loves to do, we can surreptitiously alert the authorities. There are enough of us, with enough skills that if he's got Shiva in there with him, we should be able to find it. If we can find it, we can dismantle it."

"Before he presses the launch button," Rex said.

"Hang on," I said, raising my hand to focus everyone.

The lights in Kiran's modernist house went off one by one before, minutes later, the garage door opened and a silver Tesla sports car emerged. Its headlights flickered on, and the car pulled out into the street before quickly racing away.

We sat in silence for a few minutes, waiting to see if Kiran was coming back. He did not. Five minutes after Kiran left, we exited the van and walked down the street to the front door of his Arizona mansion.

As we walked up the steps to the mansion, I warned everyone.

"Kiran knows we're coming," I said. "Whatever we find in this place, it'll likely be another lie or sales pitch to try to convince us that he's doing the right thing or to make us feel like we're so far behind we'll never have a chance of stopping him."

"But we do, right?" Teo asked.

"Of course we do," I said.

19.4

Getting in was easy.

There was no special alarm system (at least nothing out of the ordinary) and no craftily designed keys. I picked the lock while Rex and Ivan took out the surveillance cameras and motion detectors. It took us three minutes flat to get through the front door and drop ten cameras and fifteen sensors.

It certainly helped that there were seven of us. All the same, the house was not that well protected. Perhaps it was because it was a home and not a lab. Or, perhaps, we were expected.

"This feels off," I told everyone as we made our way through the massive front room of the house to the living room. The walls were essentially bare, with the exception of a handful of postmodern paintings and an odd sculpture that resembled an impressionist take on the OndScan logo.

"You think it is a trap?" Tunde asked me.

"I think it's too easy."

"Regardless," Rex said, "we're in here, we need to take a look. Dig up whatever we can, regardless of whether Kiran planted it or not."

"Where do we start?" Teo asked.

The house was three stories and at least three thousand square feet. I guessed we'd be dealing with four or five bedrooms. There would be a lot of cabinets to go through, drawers to loot, and undoubtedly computers. That was assuming Kiran kept important things at this location.

"We need to load up what we can carry, take photos of what we can't. I say we split up," I said, "ULTRA upstairs, the LODGE down."

"That's exactly how horror movies start," Rex said.

Despite Rex's joke, we all darted in separate directions. Rex and Teo headed to the living room and kitchen. Tunde took the front rooms. While I heard the ULTRA team members scrambling upstairs to the bedrooms, I walked toward the back of the house. There was a staircase leading down to the basement. As I approached it, the lights flickered on above me.

The stairs led to a wide hallway. It was lined with framed photographs. All of them highlighted Kiran with various well-known politicians and tech innovators. In each and every picture, Kiran was smiling, dressed in his finest clothes. I wasn't sure if the photographs were arranged chronologically, but at the end of the hallway there was a picture from the Game. It was of Kiran standing in the midst of the falling confetti during the Zero Hour finale. Those final minutes before everything exploded. I saw myself standing in the background of the picture. Well, **Painted Wolf** was standing there.

The hallway led to a large room. I walked inside, and, as on the stairs, the overhead lights flickered on one by one. It was an office. The walls were lined with shelves, and on the shelves were identical-looking binders, each with the OndScan logo on its side. There were computers and a bank of servers that hummed quietly on one wall. But it was the wall opposite the door to the office that had me entranced.

There was a laser display on the wall: a 3-D hologram, projected by a ceiling-mounted laser light. It was a tree and it shimmered, turning clockwise in a slow circle. I walked up to it and examined it closely, passing my fingers through its digital green branches. It was beautiful. That was when I noticed the leaves. Each had a name hovering over them. I saw General Iyabo's and Naya's names. I saw the names of the brain trusters and Game participants. I also saw the names of the ULTRA team, Terminal, and our own names: Rex, Tunde, and Painted Wolf.

Tree

"It's all there."

The voice came from behind me. I didn't have to turn around to know who it was. By now, his voice was familiar. I did turn around and saw that Kiran was standing by the door, wearing slacks and a black turtleneck shirt. He walked over to me and we shook hands, all very cordially. He didn't seem to notice that I slipped an audio bug, a tiny, sticky microphone the size of a grain of rice, onto his right sleeve.

"All the connections," Kiran said. "Each branch represents the flow of information. Each one connects the various people and projects together. I thought the image of a tree made sense, and it's got a wonderful aesthetic, don't you agree?"

"I think it's beautiful," I said.

"The tree or the plan?"

"The tree."

Kiran chuckled. "You know," he said, "I made you an offer at the Game. It still stands. If anything, I feel even more strongly now than I did before. You would make an incredible addition to my army, Painted Wolf."

"Your army is finished. You're finished. This . . ." I turned and motioned back to the laser light tree on the wall behind me. "These are all pipe dreams now. The brain trust is all but disbanded, we have the Rama code, and we'll block any move you make to launch Shiva. So there really isn't anything to join, Kiran."

He didn't seem very concerned.

"That all might be true, in some form or another," Kiran replied cryptically. "But I still have Shiva, and I still have the will to use it. But I didn't lead you, Rex, Tunde, and the kids from ULTRA all the way across the globe to confirm what you already know. I wanted you to see this and understand."

"Understand what?"

Kiran walked over to the bookshelf and removed one of the binders. He placed it on a low coffee table and removed a single sheet of paper from it. Kiran handed the paper to me. On the sheet was a typed list of dates—day, month, and year. I only recognized one of them: It was the date of the Tiananmen Square protests in Beijing.

"**This has all happened before,**" Kiran said, walking across the room toward the laser-projected tree. It spun lazily around him, the colors playing over his face and his hands. "It happened before, and it will happen again. Unless you let me do something about it."

Just then we heard Rex and Tunde at the top of the stairs. Kiran moved his hand, and the room was plunged into darkness. I didn't move, lost in the instant night, until the lights flickered on a second later.

Kiran was gone but the tree remained, endlessly spinning in place.

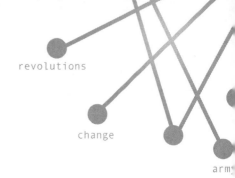

20. Rex

30 HOURS UNTIL SHIVA

We were SO close!

I can't tell you how frustrating it was walking into that basement room and hearing that I missed Kiran by less than a minute.

Teo and I searched the house and the grounds but couldn't find any trace of him. Unless he had some sort of *Phantom of the Opera* lair hidden under the place, he was likely miles away.

It was hot outside and dry enough to make my throat feel like the back of a furnace. I had no idea how people comfortably lived out in the middle of a desert.

Winded from running around, I found Cai in the living room.

She was holding a piece of paper she said Kiran gave her.

It was a list of random-looking dates.

"What's the list?" I asked, sitting beside her on a couch.

"Revolutions," Cai said. "I ran the dates. There are forty of them here, all dates of failed revolutions: times when people or groups rose up against broken or controlling systems. The only thing that really links them all is that they were crushed. Maybe things changed for a little while after these events, but, in the long run, the world went back to normal or got worse."

"That's grim."

"He wants me to know he thinks we're going to fail," Cai said. "That even if we stop him, it won't change a thing; Kiran's making fun of our revolution. He seems to think that he's the only one capable of real and effective change."

"Well, we know that's wrong."

"Do we?"

I wasn't sure where Cai was going with that, but Tunde and Stella interrupted us. They emerged from the stairs holding big duffel bags packed full with all sorts of tech, wires and cables dangling out like they'd massacred some robots.

"So what did he want?" Tunde said, setting his bag down.

"His usual," Cai said. "Wanted me to join his army."

"That what he called it?" Stella asked.

Cai nodded. "And of course, he painted the whole thing as though he'd plotted it out from the very beginning. He told me that he led us here on purpose. He didn't seem too concerned about us breaking in and finding everything."

"Well," I said, "there's a lot here."

"Yeah? What did you discover?"

"Ton of files, tons of data," Teo said, joining us from downstairs. "Place is a treasure trove of all his personal notes. They show how he developed his company, created the Game, the viruses, all of it. Only two things we don't have are access to Shiva itself and Kiran."

"Well," Cai said, winking cockily, "that's not quite true. . . ."

She showed us her cell phone and an open app. It displayed a digital recording screen, with an audio wave making peaks and valleys, and a map. There was a green dot moving toward a private airfield just a few miles away.

"Is that?!" Tunde gasped.

Cai said, "Not only can we follow him, but it has a microphone so I can hear everything he's saying."

Just to rub it in, Cai pulled a tiny earbud from her left ear.

"Have you been listening to him this whole time?" I asked.

Cai nodded.

"And I thought we were having such a nice conversation."

"Stop being silly, Rex!" Tunde shouted. "What has Kiran said?"

Cai said, "He's going to a bunker in Patagonia, Argentina."

20.1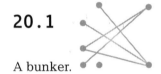

A bunker.

I'm not much of a history buff. I don't really know the first thing about battlefield strategy or offensive preparations, but I do know that people don't just throw around the word *bunker*. That's a place you go to get away from something really bad—a tornado, a fire, or a war.

Maybe Cai read it differently, but to me it meant Kiran was going to ground.

He's readying for the final battle, amigo.

"What about Shiva?" Ivan asked. "Has he said anything?"

"Nothing yet."

"We should leave," Teo said as he headed outside to the waiting van.

Seconds later we heard tires screech and Teo barreled back inside.

"Police are here!" Teo shouted. And I could see the lights

flickering through the front window as a veritable caravan of police rolled toward Kiran's modernist abode.

"Go out the back door," Teo said, pointing toward the kitchen. "There's a path to a detached garage—go around there and down the alleyway. Head to the right; the cops are coming from the north."

ULTRA ran first, Tunde and Cai following.

I paused, noticing that Teo was striding toward the front door.

"What are you doing?!" I asked him, panic rising in my throat.

"The cops are too close; you'll never get away without a distraction," he said.

"Are you kidding me?"

I grabbed my brother by the arm and spun him around to face me. Teo was calm, despite the fact that two-dozen police were seconds away from knocking down the front door.

"I just found you a few days ago, brother. I'm not going to let you do this."

"Rex." Teo pulled my hand away. "I've had this coming for a long time anyway. But you need to go. I'm really proud of you. Go stop Kiran. I'll see you soon, okay?"

As if to punctuate the moment, fists were banging on the front door.

"Go on," Teo said. "Save the world."

I hesitated, wanting to just have that one last moment with my brother. I never thought that once I'd found him I'd lose him again so quickly. But he was right: I had to stop Kiran. So I turned and ran after the others, through the kitchen, and out into the backyard toward the garage.

As I ran, I pictured the scene.

The front door to Kiran's mansion being broken down by the police, nearly off its hinges, as Teo stood stoically in the entranceway, ready to distract them with whatever story he could come up with before they slapped the cuffs on him and led him out to one of the idling police cruisers.

I was sure his story would be something great.

20.2

I ran until my lungs nearly burst.

I sped around the garage and into the alleyway. Though I couldn't see the rest of the crew, I just kept running and assumed I'd find them. The alleyway ended at an intersection. It was quiet but also empty.

I stepped out near a streetlight and caught my breath.

Okay, okay, now what?

To my left, I could see the flashing lights of the police cars. Most were piled up around Kiran's mansion, but there were several spreading out through the neighborhood. They were looking for me, and it would only be a matter of time before they found me. Sadly, I didn't have any tricks up my sleeve. No funky Tunde-tech and certainly no Cai-styled social engineering that would get me out of a run-in with the cops. Especially not while carrying a duffel full of stolen information. Nope, I was going to just have to run.

My first step was coming up with a direction.

Obviously, we'd need to get as far from the mansion as possible. Myself, I'd have just run in the opposite direction. But Cai might have chosen a different route. She might even have run toward the cops in some sort of crazy game theory ridiculousness. I'm sure she would have had a brilliant argument for it, too, but right now, I didn't feel capable of predicting her strategy.

So I decided to just run and reconnect with everyone once I got a little farther from all the chaos. I wondered what Teo was going through as I raced around a corner to my right and jumped over a series of low hedges. Was he being interrogated in the back of a squad car? What would he say to our parents when he was allowed to make a call? *If* he was allowed . . .

"Rex!"

It was Tunde. He was standing at the edge of a park next to the van. The sliding side-door was open, and ULTRA and Cai were inside. I dashed over to them.

"What happened? Where is Teo?" Tunde asked.

"He turned himself in to protect us," I said.

"I am sorry, *omo*. That was a very brave thing."

"Come on," I said. "Let's get in that van."

I jumped in and settled into a seat beside Cai as the driver hit the gas.

Cai reached over, took my hand, and squeezed it.

She understood.

21. TUNDE

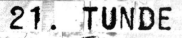

28 HOURS UNTIL SHIVA

The sacrifice that Teo made for us was truly astounding!

I have always been a sucker for tales of extreme courage. There is a story in Akika Village of a woman who bravely stood between her family and a rampaging hyena. She did not blink when the fearsome beast swiped at her face with its clawed paws. Her stoicism scared the animal off, and though she lost an eye in the attack, my people always saw the loss as a badge of honor.

While I had made many assumptions about Teo, I knew that he was truly an honorable person for what he did to secure our escape. The Teo who fell in with Terminal and considered their approach to be preferable was long gone. In Mexico City, as in Arizona, we saw the true face of Teo, and it was startlingly similar to that of my very best friend, Rex.

We reached the Phoenix airport twenty-five minutes later.

As we unloaded, Cai showed us her cell phone and the tracking app on Kiran. He was airborne, his flight headed south toward Mexican airspace.

"We have tickets?" I asked, leaning back to look at Javiera.

She nodded. "First class again."

"You are a superstar," I said. "How long is the flight?"

Cai said, "Twelve hours to Buenos Aires. Then another, shorter flight to Bariloche, a city in the Patagonia region. It'll be twenty hours give or take a few minutes. We're going to be cutting it very, very close. We'll get in just a couple hours before Shiva's launch."

"All right," Rex said. "We can go over all the stuff we've managed to gather from Kiran's and formulate a plan of attack."

I fist-bumped Rex.

"We have so much to discuss, *omo*," I said, "though I have spent only a few minutes looking at the stuff we recovered and it is all very exciting. I cannot wait to go over some of the details with you. You are going to love this."

"Tunde, your optimism is . . ."

"Is what?" I asked.

Rex laughed. "I wouldn't trade it for the world."

With that, we ran into the airport and readied for our flight. My friends, I had been traveling so much since I first left my beloved village to attend the Game that I felt as though I was now an old hand and the thrill of being on an airplane had quickly been replaced by a sort of warm familiarity.

We checked in for our flight and then passed through security.

One of the women examining IDs was Nigerian, and she and I made small talk about seeing the States and missing Naija cuisine before Rex pulled me away. We ran to our gate and boarded the plane a few minutes before takeoff.

I settled into my first-class seat alongside Stella.

She was looking through several reams of blueprints she had smuggled out of the mansion. I glanced at them with her as a steward handed us cups of black tea and water. The first of the blueprints was of the mansion itself. But a few pages in was another building, one I did not recognize. It was built into the side of a mountain.

"Do you think this might be the bunker Cai spoke of?" I asked.

Stella shrugged. "Whatever it is," she said, "it's pretty hard-core."

"How do you mean?"

Stella traced the exterior walls with her right index finger. "Do you see how thick these are? They're the kind of thing someone builds to buttress against earthquakes or maybe explosions. There's also the fact that it's three stories deep."

"Deep into the mountain?"

"Yes."

That was interesting. It meant that getting inside was going to be quite involved. I started to picture machines I could build to drill through the walls or maybe excavating equipment that could dig under them, when Stella interrupted my thoughts.

"Can I tell you something, Tunde?"

I shook myself from my planning and nodded. "Of course."

"This is new for us," Stella said. "I mean, ULTRA has been to many countries before, but our travels have always been after the fact, so to speak. We've spent our time in the shadows, gathering clues, building surveillance stuff, not actually going directly after anyone. . . ."

"So you are nervous?"

Stella nodded.

"This is understandable," I said. "When I went to the Game, I was quite anxious about every step I took. I was leaving my small village and traveling across the globe! There is simply no true way to prepare for these sorts of things. When a massive change comes, you only need to focus on yourself and ensure that you are personally ready to handle all that it may throw at you, and if you cannot handle it, then that is okay. You need to accept that."

I felt as though I was being reassuring to Stella. She had certainly proven herself many times over in Beijing, Mexico City, and Arizona. It was somewhat funny to me that she considered herself anxious now, considering all we had been through. But I supposed the thought of facing off against Kiran, the boogeyman that she had been tracking for so long, was intimidating.

Kiran he dey guy-man.

Rex tapped my shoulder.

"Tunde," he said, "come look at this."

21.1

Rex was sitting a few rows back from me with Cai and Javiera.

They all had laptops open, and were going through the materials we had acquired from the mansion in Arizona. I knelt down in the aisle beside Rex, and he spun his laptop around to show me what he had discovered.

"I think the Shiva program has a weakness," Rex said.

All I could see were long lines of code on the screen. While I may have recognized a few bits, I could not honestly say what I was looking at. Rex knew well enough that I was not a coder, but, clearly, he still wanted to show me firsthand. I have always appreciated that about Rex; he has never spoken down to me or assumed that I would not understand what he wanted to show me.

However, I did not understand it.

215

"We only have bits and pieces of the earliest drafts of Shiva," Rex said. "But lining them up and scanning through them to compare differences, I was able to find a tiny poorly designed element that Kiran, or whoever was designing this for him, overlooked through every iteration. I can't say with any certainty that it's still in the final program but . . ."

"But if it is we can take advantage of it," I said, grinning.

"Yes and no," Rex said.

"It's not really an exploitable flaw," Javiera said. "Think of it more like a seam where the two pieces that have been brought together aren't fully in line. There's a gap. It doesn't mean we can get in like a back door, but it means we can follow it just the same way we're following Kiran."

"I am not sure I understand," I said.

Rex broke it down quite simply. "Think of it like this," he said. "We can't exploit this thing and get inside the program, but when he activates it, we'll know where it's going and we can put up digital roadblocks. We can slow it."

"And this will give us time to confront Kiran," I said, comprehending the plan. "I think this is excellent. Can we block it now?"

Cai shook her head. "Not until he runs the program."

That made me a bit uncomfortable. What if Kiran were to launch Shiva and the program was immediately devastating? How could we possibly slow something that was spread out across the globe, with so many different moving pieces, in a matter of seconds? Though I was greatly appreciative of the work Rex, Javiera, and Cai did, I was not entirely convinced it would be as beneficial as they assumed. However, my friends, I would of course give them the benefit of the doubt.

"Well then," I said, "let us hope we can find him first."

I went back to my seat to find Stella and Ivan deep in a conversation. I hated to intrude, seeing that the discussion seemed rather heated, and so I walked to the front of the plane to the bathroom. Locking myself inside, I splashed water on my face, which was quite refreshing, and then had a good look at myself. My goodness! The days of running had certainly taken a toll. While I would never argue that I am a particularly handsome young man, I do believe I have several attractive attributes. A strong jawline and gentle-looking eyes. However, I had clearly lost some weight and appeared to be quite gaunt. The heavy, dark bags under my eyes attested to some significant lack of proper sleep.

I promised myself that when we had Kiran locked up and the Shiva program decimated, I would enjoy a healthy meal and a decent amount of sleep.

Returning to my seat, I discovered that the meeting between Stella and Ivan had become a full-fledged ULTRA conversation as Javiera had now joined the mix. Ivan stood up and motioned for me to retake my seat. Clearly, the conversation had been a heated one, as they all seemed quite serious.

"Tunde," Stella said, "we've made a decision."

I had not known there was a question.

"Okay," I said.

"When we get to Buenos Aires," Ivan said, "we will be staying in the city."

Javiera drove the point home. "We're not going to face Kiran with you."

21.2

I was a bit flabbergasted.

ULTRA had come this far, traveling the globe alongside us, and to think that they would not pursue the mission to the end was confusing to me. I looked back to Rex and Cai and ushered them forward. We would need to talk about this as a group. I certainly could not be the one to decide.

"I will certainly respect your decision," I told ULTRA, "but let us discuss."

I will tell you, my friends, I felt a bit bad for the people sitting in the seats alongside mine. Here they were, minding their own business on this long flight, perhaps reading their books, watching movies on tablet computers, or attempting to sleep, and suddenly a group of six young people crowd around them discussing, in whispers, all sorts of odd-sounding things.

Frankly, I am surprised no one alerted the flight crew.

Regardless, we were able to have a huddle in the center aisle.

Javiera told Rex and Cai about their decision to split off from us when we arrived in Argentina. With everyone assembled, Ivan provided more details about the decision. "To be honest with you, we've come to the conclusion that this next step is a bigger deal than we had anticipated. We're not like the

LODGE; you all are more experienced in this arena. But that doesn't mean we'll be abandoning you. While you hunt Kiran down, we will continue to go through all the information we pulled out of the mansion and focus on shutting down Shiva."

I turned to Rex to gauge his opinion of the situation.

"I can appreciate that," Rex said. "You guys have done so much for us."

Cai said, "I think it's a wise choice. Strategically, it gives us a few advantages as well. Kiran will be looking for both our groups. By splitting up, we can keep him on his toes. Also, we'll need someone on the ground watching our backs and setting up the roadblocks for Shiva if we can't."

"Okay," Ivan said. "Then it is agreed. Been fun, guys."

"It has been a wonderful experience," I said.

Stella added, "Don't anyone get teary eyed. We'll see each other soon."

We shook hands and then returned to our respective seats to continue what work we could before the plane was due to land. Looking through the odd items of technology we had removed from the mansion, Stella and I worked to modify what we could. As we were on a plane, we couldn't utilize the usual tools of our trade. No soldering irons or electric drills. We had to tweak what we could with our hands and our ingenuity. A tablet computer was easily reprogrammed to become a remote computer terminal, and a cell phone was quickly turned into a mobile microscope. I was not certain which of these items we might use in our hunt for Kiran, but it was good to have the devices readily available.

We landed at the Buenos Aires airport just before dawn.

It was really rather beautiful to see the sun cresting the horizon and illuminating the city. For a few moments, I allowed myself to be excited at the thought of visiting a new country and a new culture. Though I realized we would have absolutely no time for sightseeing, I also allowed myself the small pleasure of enjoying the landscape outside the plane window before we were thrust into the chaos of the city and the chase for Kiran.

After a tumultuous time disembarking the plane and gathering up all of our belongings, we gave a hearty farewell to ULTRA. Rex, however, pulled Javiera and Ivan aside as I spoke with Stella. I could not help but overhear the conversation they had. Rex asked them to look into trying to clear Teo. He framed it as something to do during "downtime," as though there would be any of that.

"I know he broke the law," Rex said. "I know he made some poor decisions. But I think he proved himself after Beijing. At the end of the day, he made the right choice and he did the right thing."

Ivan and Javiera agreed. They would certainly try.

Cai got an alert on her cell phone via the tracking app. It showed the bunker that Kiran had traveled to was four hours south for us—by plane to Bariloche, then by taxi and foot. Clearly, this location was not going to be easy to access. In fact, it looked quite rugged.

"Any thoughts?" Cai asked, holding up her cell.

"We're going to need some hiking boots," Rex said.

That was when all of our cell phones buzzed in our pockets.

21.3

Kiran, *ever the guy dat maja us*, had launched the Shiva program!

As expected, it immediately started to rampage through various and sundry Internet root systems across the globe. Many were instantly overwhelmed and their accounts deleted. I could only imagine the panic in the minds of the system engineers, my friends! Surely they stared at their computer screens with dread.

"Can we block it?" I asked, panic rising to a boil.

"We'll see," Rex said.

He and Javiera huddled over their cell phones and the tablet computers they had taken from the mansion on a bench near the luggage. They typed furiously as Cai and Ivan stood watch, giving advice where they could.

Stella and I did not want to stand by with our hands in our pockets.

"What can we do?" I asked Rex.

"We need to boost our signal in here," he said. "Any thoughts?"

Stella and I simultaneously looked around the baggage claim area for anything we might be able to use quickly and efficiently. Both of us focused our attention on a trash can near the exit doors. There were many metal scraps inside, including what looked like some discarded aluminum foil.

"You thinking what I'm thinking?" Stella asked me.

"Parabolic antenna," I said.

We ran as fast as we could over to the trash can and dove in with both hands, removing every scrap we thought we could use. I tell you, my friends, Stella and I must have been quite a sight! I was too absorbed in what I was doing to notice the tourists and businesspeople staring at us in bewilderment, but Stella assured me later that they most definitely were.

We returned to our friends with the aluminum foil—which

had apparently lined the bottom of a food tray or two, paper, several magazines, and a couple broken curtain rods. Though Cai and Ivan looked over at us a bit confused, hoping for an explanation, we did not have time to get into the details.

We had to build!

As Stella and I worked, Javiera updated everyone on her progress. "Here's the thing," Javiera said. "The way the virus is moving through the system, it's splitting up frequently. We need to block it at every turn. Sometimes that's easy—we throw a firewall up or reroute it into a dead end. But as this attack is developing, we're finding it more and more difficult."

"The goal for Kiran," I said with my eyes locked firmly on the project at my feet, "is to delete the Internet, correct? Then perhaps there is a way to take it off-line? The Shiva program cannot delete what it cannot find."

Rex stopped typing and looked up at me.

"That's actually a good idea," he said.

"You act surprised!" I responded. "I have a good idea every day!"

As Stella and I finished creating a parabolic antenna from the trash we had acquired, Rex and Javiera discussed putting my plan into motion. Rather than trying to block the Shiva program at every turn, they would contain it by shutting down the portion of the Internet it was rampaging through. This, of course, was certain to result in significant stress for those companies and governments using that section of the World Wide Web, but at least it would stop the damage Shiva was doing.

"We're going to do a huge distributed denial of service—a DDoS—attack on some major Domain Name System hosts," Javiera said, getting quite technical. "It's going to make people's lives miserable for a few hours, but I think it'll work in stopping Shiva. And, even better, it'll give us time to come up with a better solution."

"How's that signal boost coming along?" Rex asked.

"Done!" Stella said.

She held up our creation for everyone to see. As we had intended, it was a parabolic antenna to boost the signal of their cell phones. It looked like a funky satellite dish. Though it was square instead of circular, it wrapped around the cell phone in a half circle. The design, as well as the materials, would bounce and strengthen the signal. The parabolic antenna was not impressive to look at, but when Rex set his cell phone inside it, turned his phone onto "airplane mode," and then brought it back online, the signal was significantly boosted.

"Damn," Rex said. "That actually worked great."

"Do not act so surprised," I said. "You are dealing with prodigies here."

It took Rex and Javiera another few minutes to put their plan in motion. I was thankful that our layover between flights was a good hour; otherwise we might have missed our final push to confront Kiran. As expected, the DDoS attack went through and a good portion of the Internet was crippled. Along with it, Shiva was halted in its tracks. We all breathed a sigh of relief but knew it was to be quite short-lived as Kiran would surely find a work-around.

Kiran na coded guy.

ULTRA walked us over to the gate from which our flight would be departing. There, they confirmed again their plans to continue the attack on Shiva unabated and work with the authorities as best they could to stop it.

"You should also let the coding community know," Rex

said. "All those antivirus and security guys are going to be all over this, if they haven't already noticed."

"Done," Javiera said.

We bade farewell to ULTRA again and told them we would be in touch with them as soon as we landed in Bariloche. Boarding the plane, I was confident that we could not have left the attack on Shiva in better hands. Javiera, Ivan, and Stella were true friends and gifted revolutionaries. I knew I would be very happy when I saw them again. But there was no time for such idle musing.

We had to catch Kiran!

2.5 HOURS AFTER SHIVA

The flight was beautiful, grasslands and oceans of trees beneath us, but we were lost in our own thoughts.

Rex sat quietly beside me, his eyes on the passing clouds, and Tunde tinkered with a calculator he'd carefully taken apart.

"I've been having this nightmare thought," Rex said, turning to me. "What if Kiran discovered the tracking device you put on him, and . . . this whole thing is wrong—he's actually somewhere in Australia, about as far away as can be."

"That is a nightmare. Not going to happen, though," I said.

"I shouldn't doubt you. I'm just anxious."

"He's here, Rex," I said. "Even if he found the tracker."

"So this is a trap?"

I shook my head. "No, not for us. Kiran's ready to face us. Now that he's launched Shiva, he must know he's reached the end. This is his last stand."

Rex pondered that for a moment.

"He'd be a good guy if he wasn't **so deluded**," Rex said.

"He wouldn't be Kiran then."

Minutes after our second flight touched down in the small city, all of our cell phones buzzed with urgent messages from

ULTRA. While Shiva was still successfully stalled and some of the leading antivirus people had been alerted to Kiran's destructive program, ULTRA wasn't going to rest. With the bits of the Internet we'd shut down coming back online, it would only be a **matter of time** before Shiva was out in the open again. We had to get to Kiran before that happened.

Using the tracker's signal, we took a taxi from the small airport up winding mountain roads. There were towering pine trees and massive boulders lining the roadway, and I was a bit light-headed from the altitude. After about thirty minutes of driving we were as far removed from any signs of civilization as I'd ever been. This was a wild, raw place that gave the impression of having remained untouched since the dawn of time: the perfect spot for Kiran's bunker.

Finally, the cab came to a stop on a narrow road that cut into a mountainside. It was a beautiful but empty place. Outside of a trickling waterfall that emptied into a lake a few thousand feet below us, there was no movement and certainly no bunker visible.

"This is the place," Rex said, translating the taxi driver's Spanish.

"This cannot be the place," Tunde said. "There is nothing here."

I showed him the tracking app. According to the data on my cell screen, we were the blinking red dot about a half mile from a green triangle that signified **Kiran's bunker.** It was to our left, across the road, and straight up the mountain.

"You've got to be kidding me," Rex said, looking up through the boulders, tall grass, and towering trees toward the summit.

"How long do you think it'll take to walk, Tunde?" I asked.

Tunde looked at the map and then out at the mountainside. "Well," he said, "hard to say. Could be an hour or more." "Then we better get moving," I said.

We climbed out of the taxicab with our stuff. Rex paid the driver with the few dollars he had left and then the cab pulled out. As the sound of its grinding engine faded away, we found ourselves in the tranquil mountain silence.

22.1

I'd never been hiking before, at least not in any mountainous region like Patagonia.

Every step was tricky. The trail was heavily overgrown, and any markers that had been there were long since lost beneath the foliage. Much of the time, we had to figure out our path as we went. Sometimes we had to stop because the route was too steep; other times there was too much undergrowth or debris in the way. I assumed that Kiran traveled back and forth to his bunker via helicopter. There was simply no way he hiked up and down this mountain.

We reached a stopping point before a wall of trees. According to the tracking app, the bunker was just on the other side of the forest in a clearing.

Rex and I sat on a boulder while Tunde lay in the grass. We'd picked up some bottled water at the airport and a few bags of snacks—nuts, chips, and a chocolate bar. We shared the food, took long swigs of water, and tried to catch our breath. My calves were aching fiercely. I wasn't wearing the right shoes for a hike, and I was desperate to take them off and dip my feet into a cold mountain stream.

"Any bets on what we're going to find up here?" Rex asked.

"I just hope Kiran has the decency to offer us something warm to drink," Tunde said. "I hate to sound like a complainer, but I am exhausted."

"I would be prepared for some surprises," I said.

"Here's the thing." Rex stood and stretched. "There's no way we're going to just walk into this bunker like we did in the Arizona house. If you're right, Cai, and this is **his last stand**, then we're going to be facing off against some security."

"After all this climbing," Tunde said, "I am not sure I could do that."

"Worse comes to worst," I said, "we wait until dark."

"Um, aren't there, like, bears and stuff out here?" Rex asked.

"I am not afraid of any wildlife," Tunde said.

Rex scoffed. "Well, that's good for you, but . . ."

"Come on, guys," I said, standing. "Let's get moving."

We pushed into the trees. These were ancient hardwoods that had likely never seen the blade of an ax. They grew very close together, and the brush around them was so dense that we fell as often as we stepped. A thick fog moved in halfway through the forest, and soon we couldn't see more than fifteen feet ahead.

"This is unbelievable," Rex said. "Could it get any worse?"

"Of course it could," Tunde said. "I am sure there are bears in here."

I told them both to just keep their heads down and keep moving.

A half hour later, we stepped out of the woods and into a wide clearing. Tall grass, the height of my shoulders, stretched off toward a glass and stone building sitting in the middle of the open space. It looked like something that had dropped down from space. The contrast between the wild nature surrounding the bunker and its postmodernist, geometric design was striking.

Kiran's Argentine bunker

We moved low through the grass, making sure to walk in a line as silently as possible. When we were within a hundred feet of the bunker, I motioned for the boys to come up alongside me. There were **no sign of guards or security of** any kind. I couldn't even see cameras on the exterior of the bunker.

"So much for the security," Rex whispered. "What's up with this?"

"I don't know," I said. "Maybe we're missing something."

Tunde scanned the exterior of the building carefully and

then pointed to the roof. "There is his transport," he said. We all moved toward Tunde to see Kiran's helicopter sitting on the roof. It was the same one he'd used in Nigeria.

Seeing it, knowing that Kiran was certainly here, I sent word to ULTRA to alert the authorities to our location. We needed them en route and fast. I also gave them the passwords to access the live feeds from the button cameras on my clothes and gear. If they could see what we were seeing, they'd be there all the sooner.

"You're the expert on the whole break-in thing," Rex said, turning to me.

I thought for a few seconds as wind whistled through the treetops and somewhere in the distance a bird called. Then I looked again at the tracking app. The green arrow was blinking inside the building sitting before our eyes.

Kiran was in there, waiting for us.

"Follow me," I said.

22.2

We crept around the exterior of the bunker carefully.

I was shocked at the absence of any visible alarm systems. I've prided myself on being able to make out even the smallest of camera and sensor systems. I couldn't see any on the bunker, but I was sure they were there. The edges were seamless, as though the place were designed to be a sculpture placed in a garden.

"This building is so remote," Tunde whispered. "Perhaps Kiran never thought to install protection for it?"

"Doesn't sound like Kiran," I said.

We passed by several windows, and I peeked into the

rooms. Nothing much to look at besides drab colors and modern furniture, but I was wrong about the security. Sure enough, the place looked like a bank vault. I saw tiny corner-mounted cameras, motion sensors, and microwave sensors.

"Damn," I said to the boys. "Exterior's light on tech, but inside, it's insane."

"So what's our play?" Rex asked.

"We find a room we can break into," I said.

We made our way to a glass sliding door on the north side of the bunker. Looking inside, we could see a reading room with carefully organized shelves lining the walls and low, modernist furniture. The room was empty and the lights were off. I did not see any visible cameras or motion detectors.

I tried the handle on the sliding door. It was locked.

"Well, at least he's locking the doors," I said.

I pulled my lock pick from my pants pocket and picked the lock. But just before I opened the door, I saw it: A thermal infrared sensor was positioned on the ceiling of the room. It would have 360-degree coverage, and there was no way to dodge it once we were past the glass.

Unless . . .

I turned back to Tunde. "Can you help me make a blanket of leaves?"

"What?" Tunde looked shocked.

"Nothing fancy," I said. "We need to weave together leaves. The biggest we can find. Just enough to cover me as I go into this room."

Being in a South American forest gave us some significant advantages. For one, there were dozens of types of large leaves readily available. Within a few minutes, we'd gathered together enough leaves—some as large as my head—to make a sort of blanket by weaving them stem to stem. It wasn't perfect, and if anyone had seen me drape it over myself, I'd have been instantly committed.

But I figured it would work.

"What exactly does this do?" Rex asked.

"The infrared sensor can't see through the leaves," I said. "If I can sneak in, cross the room, then hit the power, I can shut it down and we can move inside."

I slid open the door and then crept into the room under the leaf blanket. It was slow going; I couldn't move too quickly in case the blanket unraveled. Also, I didn't want any of my skin to be exposed and set off the sensor. My heart was pounding in my ears as I practically crawled across the floor. The muscles in my legs and neck ached. But it worked. I was able to cross the room into a nearby hallway.

There, I found an outlet I was able to pry from the wall using my lock pick. Once I had it free, I was able to short the power to the room. The thermal infrared sensor flickered once and then went dull.

I threw off the leaf blanket and motioned to the boys.

They crossed the room wearing big grins.

"Never seen that before," Rex whispered.

We were in a narrow hallway. In the distance, we could hear voices over the rush of the forced air. It sounded like a television was playing somewhere in another part of the bunker.

Following the sound, we moved down the hallway. The walls were lined with large, framed blueprints and technical papers. As we passed by, Rex pointed one out to me. It was the specs for a camera to be mounted on a drone. It took me a few seconds to realize it was the same camera associated with my father's company. Farther down the hallway we saw a technical paper about the processing of tantalum from Nigeria for use in tablet computers.

The hallway led to a large atrium with a glass ceiling. There were dozens of potted trees and a fountain at the center of the room. Koi fish swam in lazy circles at the fountain's base. Off to the side of the fountain were several robotic prototypes, machines that looked like more advanced versions of the equipment we created for the Game. While Tunde looked more closely at the robots, Rex stood by the fountain.

"This is unbelievable," Rex said. "A little bit of paradise, huh?"

We moved farther into the bunker, down a longer hallway.

"Listen," I told the guys. "When we find Kiran, let me do the talking. I think I know the final move in this chess game."

"We've got your back," Rex said.

Tunde nodded. "Just signal if you need us."

At the end of the hallway, the distant voices we'd heard when we walked in were much louder. From the sound of them, they were indeed from a television.

In fact, at the end of the hallway we found a second atrium, though this one was lined with television screens. They sprouted up on stands in a massive ring, like a circular window onto every corner of the world. As we stepped inside, we noticed that the TVs were tuned to various news outlets, live-blogging feeds, and web forums. All of them displayed up-to-the-second reports on the discovery of the Shiva program, the revolt of the brain trust, the collapse of OndScan, and the search for Kiran Biswas, wanted on dozens of international criminal charges.

"First row seats to the fall . . ."

Kiran's voice emerged from behind us, and we all turned to see him walk into the room holding a mug of hot chocolate. He was dressed down, wearing jeans and a hoodie. It was strange seeing him in clothes I normally associated with Rex. I couldn't tell if he looked defeated in his getup or even more smugly confident.

"Don't worry," Kiran said. "There are **no guards here**. No alarms."

He sat down in a leather chair across from us.

"Please," he said, motioning to several couches. "Have a seat."

I chose to stand. So did Rex and Tunde.

"Come on," Kiran said. "We're old friends. Don't make this more uncomfortable than it already is. When you broke in here, I almost thought that maybe you'd finally come around to see my side of things. But looking at your faces, your expressions, I can tell you still haven't caught on. I've always said I expected more from the LODGE . . . especially you, Painted Wolf."

While Rex and Tunde remained standing, I walked to a chair near one of the television screens and then dragged it closer to Kiran.

I turned it around and sat on it backward, eye to eye with him.

"I finally figured out what this is all about," I said.

"Oh," Kiran chuckled, "you did, huh? Please tell me."

"Validation," I said.

Kiran looked bemused. "You think I did this to . . . impress people?"

"No," I said. "You did this to impress us. And it worked."

"I'm confused," Kiran said.

I motioned to the television screens displaying Kiran's failure. According to the news crawls that I could see, the Shiva program was being dismantled quickly. Though it had done significant damage to certain sectors, it was not as widespread as intended. Then there was the brain trust; our information packet had worked. They'd rebelled entirely, all of them abandoning Kiran en masse.

"You orchestrated the perfect audition," I said.

"I did? For what?"

I let the mystery hang for a moment, playing Kiran's own game.

"Unfortunately, you've had it backward this whole time," I continued. "You've been trying to win us over to your side and failing, honestly, because you didn't have the one thing that I—that all of us—were looking for: compassion. You've been leading with ideas first and heart second. Ideas won't change the world, Kiran. Computer programs won't, either. People will. Admit that, and you'll have finally passed the audition."

"What the hell are you talking about?" Kiran said, looking panicked.

I smiled. "It's time for you to **join the LODGE**."

Kiran laughed nervously. "You have to be kidding me!"

"Not at all. That's what you've wanted all along, right? The brain trust, the black box labs, Shiva and Rama, all were designed to make you feel like a part of something. You've been looking for a family, and you figured that a cause, a noble cause, might be the way to get you there. But your ego did you in. Now that everything has crumbled, I think it's time for you to start over. We'd like to give you a chance to do that with the LODGE."

Kiran shook his head. "This is silly. . . ."

"We could really use someone like you on the team, Kiran."

"Enough!" he said. "You ruined something incredible. If you had let Shiva do its thing, the outcome would have been glorious. It doesn't matter now. You probably thought you could track me down here and . . . what? Pull off a citizen's arrest or something? I'm sorry to disappoint you, but I have dozens of bunkers like this across the globe. Even though I don't have the brain trust or OndScan anymore, I do have one luxury. I have time . . . all the time I need to rebuild and come back even stronger."

Kiran picked up a remote from the coffee table and turned off the TV screens.

"I'm going to leave now," Kiran said. "You'll be hearing from me."

"Actually, you're wrong," I said. "Time is the one thing you don't have."

Kiran narrowed his eyes.

"We weren't the only ones tracking you," I said.

22.3

There was a loud crash as the atrium's glass ceiling shattered.

Soldiers carrying weapons descended into the room from ropes, some of them landing with splashes in the fountain, before cornering Kiran. The soldiers shouted for him to get on his knees and put his hands over his head. Kiran obliged them, carefully kneeling as he was handcuffed.

Tunde could not help himself and clapped loudly.

"You see!" he shouted at Kiran. "As I have always warned you, this is what happens when you mess with the LODGE!"

One of the soldiers helped Kiran to his feet.

A man in a double-breasted suit and a bright green tie walked into the atrium from another part of the house. He wore glasses, had dark skin, carried a single file folder, and had a thick South African accent.

"Well done," he said to me.

We shook hands.

"I'm with Interpol," the man in the suit continued. "I assume you're Painted Wolf? And your associates here are members of the LODGE?"

I nodded and then pointed to Rex and Tunde.

"We're the LODGE."

"My name is Lethabo Reddy," the man said. "I am here to take Kiran into custody and work with you to clear your names. I realize you traveled incredible distances to get to this point. I have sightings of you across the globe. Someone even told me they'd picked up your trail in Beijing a few days ago. Regardless of whether that is true or not, we can help to make everything right again."

Tunde said, "Thank you, sir. That is all we have wanted."

Mr. Reddy opened his files and read through them quietly for a moment.

"This is the matter of New York, however," Mr. Reddy said. "I understand that you all essentially broke Mr. Huerta out of custody. Then gave the police quite a time running around the streets before you vanished on a flight to Nigeria. Is that true?"

Rex said, "That's true."

"And the computer program, WALKABOUT, did you design that?"

Rex nodded. "But I didn't use it to raid banks. Kiran did that."

"You did, however, use it to access multiple government databases, thousands of commercial and organizational cameras, and trillions of bytes of privately-held data in a search for Mr. Teo Huerta. Is that correct?"

"Yes," Rex said. "I was looking for my brother."

Mr. Reddy replied with a curt "Um-hmm."

"We were doing the only thing we could," I said. "No one would listen, and Kiran framed us to appear guilty. The only way out was to run and **prove our innocence** ourselves. Ask Kiran, he'll tell you."

"We certainly will," Mr. Reddy replied. Then he turned back to the file in his hands. "And the business with the general in Nigeria? You were also behind that?"

Tunde raised his hand. "We were defending my village."

"How about the balloon stuff in Mexico City?"

Rex said, "That was pretty much all of us."

Mr. Reddy closed his file and then put his arms behind his back and looked us over carefully. We were muddy from the hike and exhausted from weeks of running and sleep-deprivation. Now that it was effectively over, it was hard for me to see the next move. I'd been so focused on stopping Kiran that the strategy beyond his takedown was pretty cloudy. I knew we would likely face some repercussions, but I had no idea what they might be. The last thing I wanted to feel in this moment of celebration was anxiety. Kiran, oddly enough, was the first to speak.

"I pushed them," he said. "I pushed them harder than anyone has before."

"What do you mean by that?" Mr. Reddy asked.

"Before me," Kiran said, his hands shifting uncomfortably in the cuffs, "they were at seventy, maybe eighty, percent of their potential. Rex was good but not memorable. Tunde was brilliant but isolated. Painted Wolf . . . well, Painted Wolf was gifted and driven, but she let her moral compass drive her decisions. They were a loose team, a group of friends. After me, they are a force to be reckoned with. I did what I had to do to make them what they are right now."

I actually laughed. Mr. Reddy turned and looked at me as though I'd been disrespectful. "It is true that we weren't as close or as focused before the Game," I told Kiran. "But that had nothing to do with your plans or ambitions. We came together to stop you and actualized our own potential to do it. You were a good adversary, Kiran. But I think you overestimate us, and your downfall was your own. As we say in China, if you do not change your direction, you're likely to end up where you're headed."

"Okay," Mr. Reddy said. "Take him out."

Mr. Reddy motioned for the soldiers holding Kiran. The glass crunched on the floor beneath their boots as they began leading Kiran away.

"What will happen to him?" Rex asked Mr. Reddy.

He said, "I shouldn't be telling you this, but . . . since you've been open with me . . . Mr. Biswas will be put to work. There is no sense in throwing him in a cell and letting that clever mind of his just rot. No, he needs to clean up the mess he's made and use his gifts for productive, constructive purposes."

"You can't trust him," I began.

Mr. Reddy interrupted me with a wave.

"Of course," he said. "Mr. Biswas will be placed in a secure location without contact to any networks or the Internet. His work will be on analog devices, mostly good old pen and paper. I assure you that he will be cared for properly, but I also assure you that he will not be free to pursue any private ambitions for a very, very long time. My sincere hope is that Kiran can become the person the world has always hoped he would be."

We all watched quietly as Kiran was taken out of the bunker. Through the windows we could see him being led by the soldiers across the open space toward a military helicopter. He ducked his head as he slipped inside. It was strange watching this scene play out and recalling how only a little bit ago I'd watched Kiran and Rex climb into a helicopter in Nigeria. Then, while I was mostly confident that everything would work out, I secretly worried my conviction would fail. Now I was watching everything we'd hoped for come to fruition. I can't tell you how happy I felt seeing that helicopter lift off and then disappear into the sky. It was like an entire mountain range had been knocked from my shoulders.

I looked over at Rex, and he looked at me and smiled.

"We did it," he said. "We did it."

22.4

"So what happens to us now?" Rex asked me.

"I'm not sure," I said.

"That's a first."

We were standing outside Kiran's bunker as the sun sank behind the mountain peaks. While Mr. Reddy and the soldiers spent time walking through the building, cataloging and photographing everything, he allowed us time to make a few calls with our cells.

I called ULTRA first.

Javiera answered and screamed into the phone so loud I

had to hold it away from my head for a moment. She told me she'd been watching the live feeds from my cameras. She'd seen the whole thing. Javiera asked when they'd see us next, and I told her it'd be soon, but I had no idea if that was true.

As Rex called his parents and Tunde called home to Akika Village, I stepped away and rang my mother. She answered on the third ring, confused about the phone number that had shown up on her cell.

"Mother," I said, "it's me. Everything is okay. It's over."

She sighed, and I could hear the great relief in her voice.

"Where are you? Are you coming home?"

"Soon, Mother. Soon."

Mr. Reddy stepped out of the bunker and walked over to us. He pulled out the file folder he'd been looking at earlier. Reading it over silently, he took a pen from his pants pocket and made a few scribbles before looking back up at us.

"Here's the deal," Mr. Reddy said. "We can't exactly just let you three waltz back into the lives you had before this whole adventure. First, it would set a bad precedent. But, more importantly, I don't think the lives you had before would work anymore. At least not the way they were."

Mr. Reddy turned to Rex.

"I understand you effectively ghosted your parents' status recently?"

Rex nodded. "I did."

"We will have to deal with that later, but for now, we've worked things out with the Americans and you'll be returning home to California. The FBI would like to meet with you in the next couple days to discuss your legal situation as well as make an offer. I'll leave it to them to explain the details of that."

Mr. Reddy focused his attention on Tunde next.

"Mr. Oni," he said, "you will be flown back to Akika Village. I will join you on the journey, as I have business in Nigeria. I've heard rumors of a celebration in your village, and I'm eager to see what they've planned. I hope, on the way, that you and I can have a conversation about some of the technology you've developed. Our organization certainly has some open spots for minds like yours."

Tunde nodded. "I would be more than happy to talk, but more than that, I would be absolutely delighted to have you come tour my beautiful Akika Village and meet my proud and incredible people."

Lastly, Mr. Reddy turned to face me.

"Painted Wolf," he began, "amazingly, you've somehow managed to leave the fewest bread crumbs of the group. We don't know much about you, but I suspect you'd like to keep it that way. Our friends at the Chinese embassy are familiar with your work. Some of it they're willing to turn a blind eye to; some of it they'd rather talk with you about in more detail. Regardless, you'll be flown back to Beijing from Buenos Aires this evening."

Mr. Reddy then spoke to all of us as a group.

"You've done excellent work here," he said. "I don't think anyone at Interpol would agree with all the tactics you used, but the end result was impressive. You managed to not only stop the most dangerous technological threat we've faced since the Internet age began, but you led us to the mastermind behind it. For that, we thank you. I'll give you all a moment to say your good-byes."

Mr. Reddy stepped back, and Rex and Tunde walked over to me. We all hugged and laughed. Though we all had things to say, we didn't speak. We just looked at each other, eyes dancing with emotion, and smiled.

We might be separating for now, but we knew this wasn't the end of the LODGE.

I walked with Rex to the waiting helicopter.

We held hands as we walked, no longer caring if anyone saw us together.

After we'd strapped into our seats, Rex and I kissed.

"Even though it was tense and crazy and there were moments there where I thought everything was going to fall apart," Rex said, "I'd **do it all over** again in a heartbeat just so I could spend time with you."

"So would I."

Tunde climbed in beside me and put his arm around my shoulder.

The helicopter lifted off and began its winding way down the mountain before vanishing into the low clouds.

Shouting over the turbines, Tunde said, "We have done an amazing thing here! When we were inside the bunker, I could not help but watch the screens on the walls. What I saw was exactly what we had wanted: a revolution. A revolution of young people, some of them prodigies but a lot of them not, using their talents to protect their world and change their stars. It was **a glorious thing.**"

"It's not over, Tunde," I replied.

Tunde beamed.

I said, "It's just begun."

FOUR MONTHS LATER

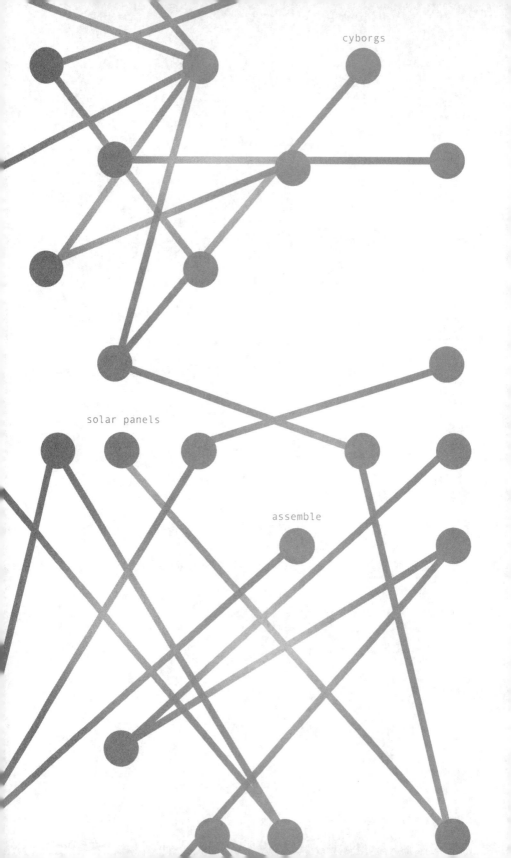

cyborgs

solar panels

assemble

23. Rex

"No," I told Tunde, "that's not going to work."

We were sitting at a large desk beside each other, both wearing virtual reality headsets that made us look like cyborgs. Tunde had wired gloves on that allowed him to manipulate digital objects in his field of vision.

Though our bodies were in California, we were looking at a rural village in Bangladesh. It was beautiful, surrounded by jungles. We could even see the ocean in the distance, sparkling and cobalt blue.

Tunde was attempting to assemble a computer-generated solar composting machine—it looked like a silver cube the size of a doghouse—in a clearing between two houses. He was totally struggling with the solar panels for the top.

"You need to move it to the other side," I told Tunde.

"You think this is so easy? You assemble it."

We were working on our latest LODGE program, which we'd dubbed Project Solar. The goal was to build solar composting machines in rural villages across Southeast Asia. We'd gotten funding from a large multinational, and the first of the machines was due to ship in a few weeks.

There was a team in Bangladesh called the ALLIANCE, and they'd set up the augmented-reality live stream we were watching through our headsets. ALLIANCE, like ULTRA and the dozen other teams we were currently running on various projects across the globe, were young people eager to make big changes in the world.

Unlike ULTRA, they were not prodigies.

Just regular kids—three girls, one from Tasmania, one from Italy, and one from Bangladesh—who impressed us with their passion and quick-wittedness. It didn't matter that they weren't taking biochemistry at age eight. They were self-taught coders or engineers, and they thought of incredible things every day.

There was a knock on the door.

"Come on in," I said.

The door opened, and Alfonso, from the Mexico City black box lab, walked in with a tray filled with random computer components. He had been working with several other brain trust members from Mexico City to design a waterproof tablet computer for a project we had going in Mauritius.

Alfonso set the tray down on the desk.

"How's it going?" he asked.

Tunde groaned. "Rex is making this difficult."

"Well, today's a special day," Alfonso said. "Maybe you want to take a break from that until tomorrow. Don't need to have that up and perfected until next month anyway."

"Yes," Tunde said. "But I hate to leave things half-finished."

I took off my VR headset and stood and stretched.

"Everyone else still here?" I asked Alfonso.

"A few of them have left, but there's a meeting going on in the conference room," he said. "You want to come down and listen in for a minute? They're talking about that self-driving car tech from the India lab."

248

I slapped Tunde on the back and told him I was leaving.

"You should finish tomorrow," I said.

"Fine. Fine," he said. "But I really do not like—"

"Leaving things half-finished," I said. "We all know."

Tunde and I followed Alfonso down the hall to the conference room where fifteen of the LODGE members had gathered. It was a sunny room, designed so that the big windows looked out over the desert and got as much sunlight as possible every day.

The fifteen people in the conference room were all former brain trust members—some from Kolkata, some from Beijing, and a bunch from Mexico City. Tunde and I took a seat quietly so we didn't interrupt the conversation.

Truth is: I didn't listen that carefully.

I sat down and looked around the room and was again amazed at how quickly our grand plan had come together. After taking down Kiran in Argentina, I returned home to face the legal music. Considering how many laws I'd broken—I'd had no idea there were so many—I'd gotten off fairly easily. Instead of the jail time I'd half expected, I was asked to issue a formal apology and then work for the government until my debt to society was paid off. And while that sounds pretty boring, my new government job turned out to be something kind of amazing.

Inspired by the results of Kiran's black box labs, I was allowed to refurbish an abandoned government lab in the middle of the Californian desert—can't tell you where 'cause it's highly classified—and, under government supervision of course, bring in my own team to run programs like the two I mentioned.

Basically, I was given the chance to continue the LODGE's work but expanded in crazy new ways. Tunde, Cai, and I recruit geniuses and passionate young people from all across the world to make a difference.

Sometimes that difference is here in the United States; most of the time it's not. Sometimes it involves environmental work—like creating a swarm of small bots to locate land mines in the leaf litter of a Zambian forest—and sometimes it's about spreading information—like the drone library we operate in Yellowknife.

We were doing amazing work.

Work all of us were incredibly proud of.

But every now and then we needed a break, and to take time to celebrate.

Don't you?

LODGE lab

23.1

We left the LODGE facility—don't really have a better name yet—and headed home.

Tunde and I rode our bicycles because we lived only a few blocks away.

My parents had just finished construction on a duplex house. It wasn't anything major, three bedrooms each, but it was new and we could call it ours. My family had moved into one side of the duplex and next door . . . Tunde's family.

Crazy, right!?

With the LODGE going wide, I couldn't exactly run the show by myself. So I called in Tunde and Cai. It was difficult for Tunde to consider coming all the way to California. Though he wanted to stay with his people in Akika Village, he realized that this was an opportunity to make real change and didn't want to miss it.

His parents agreed to move with him.

So now my best friend was my neighbor.

We arrived at the duplex and went over to Tunde's side first. The living rooms of both houses were still stacked high with boxes.

We'd only moved in a couple weeks earlier.

Tunde gave me a quick tour of the modifications he'd made on his bedroom. He'd set up a workstation in one corner with a CB radio; he had what looked to me like a junk pile under his bed (he insisted it was parts he'd scavenged for a bio-fuel engine); and he was prepping to do something with a hydroponics system for a project we had in Yemen.

Typical Tunde. Always planning ten things at once.

A car horn sounded outside, and I knew exactly who it was.

"Come on, Tunde," I said, grabbing his sleeve. "Reunion time."

We ran down the stairs and out into the street to find a ride-sharing car idling in front of my house. The front passenger door opened, and Teo stepped out. I gave him a great big hug. He messed up my hair—which I'd cut recently, shorter than usual—and then waved to Tunde before he closed the car door and thanked the driver.

"Welcome home, brother," I said. "What do you think?"

Teo surveyed the duplex and nodded.

"What're we going to do with all this room?"

"I set you up in the basement," I said. "Moved all your stuff down there. I know you like having your peace-and-quiet space. Hope you dig it."

"I'm sure I will. Folks inside?" Teo asked.

"Yeah," I said. "Mama's cooking up a storm."

"Can't wait. Tunde, you joining us?"

Tunde shook hands with Teo.

"It is a true delight to see you again, *omo*," Tunde said. "My parents and I will be joining you for dinner. My parents are planning to bring along egusi soup, one of my very favorite dishes. You will love it; it is made with fermented beans and fish."

"Awesome," Teo said. "The food in prison was . . . well, not good."

Teo and I walked to the front door together.

"You got all my letters?" I asked.

"Read them each two, maybe three times. You guys . . .
I can't even tell you how impressed I am with what you did.
Not only did you stop Terminal but Kiran's in prison. That's all
thanks to you and your team. Incredible."

I put my arm over Teo's shoulders.

"Couldn't have done it without your sacrifice, brother."

"Maybe . . ."

"Come on," I said. "It's time to celebrate. Head on inside
and say hi."

Teo went into the house with Tunde. I stayed outside
because I could hear the hiccuping engine of a scooter
approaching. Twenty-two seconds later, Cai rounded the
corner on her black Peugeot Iceblade. Helmet and leather
riding gloves on, she looked as effortlessly cool as ever.

Cai pulled the scooter into the driveway. Then she got off,
took off her helmet, and gave me a bit of a shock. I hadn't seen
her for about a week—she'd been traveling in the Caribbean
to interview a new LODGE team—and wasn't expecting much
of a change.

"What do you think?" she asked, running her fingers
through her blue hair.

Yeah, blue.

"I love it," I said. "Can't imagine it helps with blending in,
though."

Cai laughed. "I'm just in for the night. Thought I'd have fun."

"Come over here."

She did and we kissed. Her hair was not only shocking
blue but it smelled like fresh citrus. I couldn't get enough of
the scent. I hadn't realized we'd been kissing for as long as we
had until Papa cleared his throat behind me.

"Dinner's ready," he said.

Suddenly embarrassed, I turned beet red and said, "Papa. Cai's here."

"I noticed. Come on, food's going to get cold."

We were having dinner early because it was going to be a huge meal. Ma had gone nuts in the kitchen, and Cai and I walked in to find a good half-dozen dishes already on the table. We sat down next to each other, Teo on my right, Tunde on Cai's left. It was amazing seeing us all sitting at that table, crammed in together.

Tunde's parents alongside my parents.

My best friend and my girlfriend sitting with my brother.

How could anyone ask for more?

We ate until our stomachs were near to bursting. Seriously. I had to kick back my chair from the table just to stop myself from having another serving of this or that. Tunde's parents made this incredible dessert with plantains that I couldn't get enough of. It was embarrassing. As the meal wound down, Teo told us he'd heard news about Kiran. An old Terminal pal had an insider at Interpol.

"Apparently," Teo said, "he's up to amazing things."

"Yeah?" I said. "Like what?"

"Going back to his guru roots," Teo said. "He's been writing these inspirational essays that have been popping up on social media. I don't know how he's getting them out of wherever they're keeping him—"

Cai said, "I warned them."

"Anyway," Teo continued, "a few of the other hackers I met while I was . . . *incarcerated* were familiar with his work. Apparently, he's preaching a new gospel of change and transformation. I didn't read any of the essays he'd written, but they were all about making a new life for yourself and discovering the true nature of the world via minimalism and stripping away technology."

"That doesn't sound like our Kiran," I said.

Teo shrugged. "Maybe it isn't, but I like to think the guy has an interesting second life. Reinventing himself as a champion of analog technology is pretty clever if you ask me. And who knows, it just might work."

We all mulled that over.

Tunde said, "In my country we have a saying: 'No matter how dark it is, the hand will always know its way to the mouth.' Kiran is the same way. It is in his nature to always create. So long as his creations benefit humanity and this world, I think we should take them seriously. If we ever meet him again and he truly has changed as you say he has, I would gladly shake his hand."

Tunde looked to me and gave one of his classic smiles.

"You're a good person, Tunde," I said. "And you make us all better."

Tunde shrugged. *"Wit the LODGE everything be yori yori."*

23.2

After dinner, Cai and I took a long walk to the LODGE facility.

We climbed up onto the roof to look out at the stars.

Being far from most of the large cities, the sky was clear and you could see a lot of the Milky Way. Not the fine detail that you get in photos but enough of the density of stars that it gave the night sky a shimmering look.

Four months after our time in Argentina it felt a bit crazy

to be sitting, literally, on the fruits of our labor. We had the LODGE building, and the LODGE program was something we'd only ever dreamed of doing. The revolution that Tunde had envisioned had become a reality—there were now a dozen teams of young people across the planet doing incredible things to lift themselves and their communities out of poverty, out of ignorance, and out of persecution.

And yet, there was one downside.

Cai would be leaving in the morning.

She was the voice of our movement, the face of our revolution.

Before we were even the LODGE, Cai was out there exposing corruption and persecution. She wasn't going to stop that just because we'd taken down Kiran. No, that was just one step in a much larger goal.

Truth is: There are many more Kirans out there.

Cai, of course, was determined to get them all.

As we sat on the rooftop of the LODGE facility, Cai sighed and took my hand.

"It's a big world out there," Cai said. "Gets lonely."

"You weren't lonely before," I joked.

"I wish you could come with me," Cai said. "You can code anywhere."

We'd discussed this before, when she was in Russia a few weeks back, and I'd considered asking to transfer over to Interpol or something so I could go as well, but there was just so much going on at the LODGE facility that I wouldn't feel right leaving yet, even if I had been allowed to.

"I know," I said. "And I will, later, once I'm eighteen, legally allowed to leave the country, and we've got all this set up properly. In the meantime . . ."

I reached into the pocket of my hoodie and pulled out a small package.

Even though I'd planned this for weeks, my heart was racing.

"I have something for you," I said, handing it to Cai.

It was a small box, the size of an index card. I couldn't find any wrapping paper in the house—likely it was still boxed up somewhere—so I had to use newspaper. I picked the weather page because of the colors.

Cai looked the box over. "What is this?" she asked.

"Well," I said, "you have to open it to find out."

She tore off the paper carefully, which was silly, considering I'd pretty much used scraps. Then Cai looked over at me. I was anxious enough about her seeing what was inside; her gaze made my heart race even more.

Cai opened the box.

Inside was a pendant I'd made for her. It was an oval with several spirals circling a central geometric shape. Very simple. She lit up seeing it.

"What does it mean?"

"It means strength and companionship," I said. "It's a bit of Aztec, a bit of my own design. I wanted a way to be with you no matter where you go. I was hoping you'd wear it and think of me, and, well . . ."

I reached over and picked up the pendant.

Pushing on a latch on the small pendant's side unlocked the front. It was a case, and inside was a sesame-seed-sized radio frequency identification (RFID) blocker. "Tunde and I designed it. It detunes the RFID signals from any credit cards or ID cards you might have. So if anyone tries to scan you without your knowledge, this little thing will stop it. When you press here"—I pressed on the top of the pendant—"it turns it off or on. That way, you're protected from spies."

Cai looked down at the pendant, then leaned over, eyes closed, and kissed me.

"I love it," she said.

"I wanted it to be functional."

"It's perfect."

We sat on the roof, hand in hand, staring up at the spinning stars above us, for the next hour. Around nine, Cai said it was time she got going. She had to be at the airport a couple hours before her flight to Greece since she was packing so much tech for this next leg of her travels.

We climbed down from the roof and walked back toward my house.

There, Cai gathered up her helmet and gear; said good-bye to Mama and Papa, Tunde's parents, Tunde, and Teo; and then walked outside with me to her scooter.

"Call me as soon as you get in," I said.

"Of course," Cai replied.

As she got onto her scooter and started the engine, I said, "I think we'll have this whole compost thing figured out in the next week or so. Then there's the ULTRA project in Belize. But after that, I think I'll meet you somewhere virtually with the augmented reality setup. Where will you be at the end of the month where we have a cam?"

Cai flipped up the visor on her helmet.

"Iceland."

"I love Iceland," I said. "See you there."

She blew me a kiss, waved to everyone standing in the windows watching us from the house, and then sped off.

As I watched her scooter vanish into the night, I couldn't help but feel a wave of satisfaction wash over me. We'd done it. We'd accomplished our goals and changed our stars. Not only were we working hard and having fun making the world a better place, but we were doing it all together.

We are the LODGE, a team, a family.

And we're creating our own future.

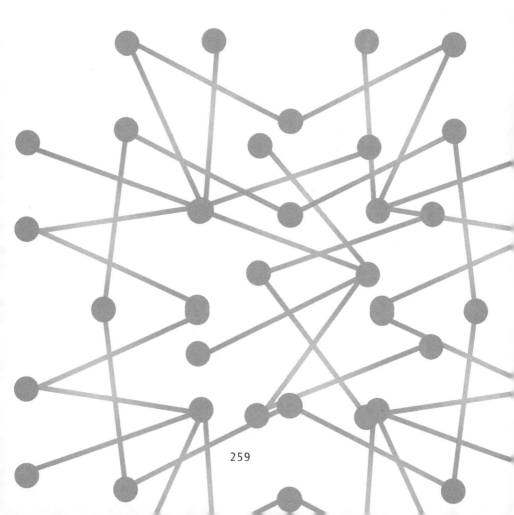

From: Rex_n_effex@lodge_revolution.com
Subject: Where are you?

Isaac Newton once said, "Genius is patience."

He's right, of course. The one thing that really separates prodigies from the rest of the world is time. Some of us, like myself and my LODGE companions Painted Wolf and Tunde Oni, start early. They label us geniuses because we can do impressive things at a young age, but that doesn't mean you can't as well.

It's all relative (a time pun, sorry).

Like I said when this all started, they call us "special," but we're still like you. We go to the beach, we get in fights with our friends, we have long-distance romances, and we wish we could draw better. We also just happen to have brains that the white coats have dubbed "organic computers." Wasn't like we chose to be this way, though.

The world is a different place now than it was the first time I wrote you. No, the sky hasn't turned pink and the moon isn't made of plastic. Not that sort of different. What's different is that there are so many opportunities now. When we began this adventure—it feels like the Game was forever ago!—we only had ourselves to rely on. Now we have you, and that makes all the difference. You are going to lead us toward something incredible. . . .

Like I said last time, the world our parents grew up in is history. All the old rules, we've thrown them out. We're the ones making the future. We're the founding fathers. Hand us universal Wi-Fi and soup dumplings, and we'll fix the world.

So how do you fit in? What if you can't code? What if you've never been able to build anything more than a birdhouse? It doesn't matter. You've got skills that you probably dismiss as tricks. That dance you can do, that song you can sing, the painting hanging in your room, those are all skills we need.

See, there's a reason my status online is: *Recruiting for the future.*

We broke some eggs and we baked a cake. It was delicious, really amazing cream cheese frosting. I saved you a piece, but I don't want to give it to you. I want to teach you how to bake your own cake from scratch. Only, instead of flour and water and eggs, I want you to make something with oil paints, yarn, peptides, or computer parts.

The revolution is now. Welcome aboard. And, uh, get ready to create. . . .

See ya,
Rex Huerta

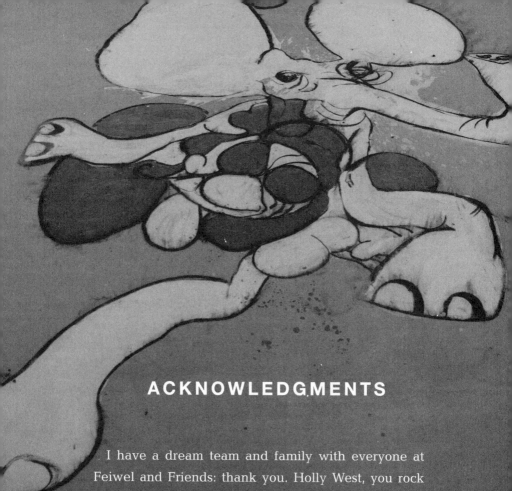

ACKNOWLEDGMENTS

I have a dream team and family with everyone at Feiwel and Friends: thank you. Holly West, you rock my world.

I'm also eternally grateful to Keith Thomas, my wonderful partner with whom I'm creating endless worlds and wild adventures.

Thank you to my family & friends—you know who you are.

To Brian David Johnson and everyone at Arizona State University Center for Science & the Imagination, where we will continue this adventure: http://csi.asu.edu/fellows-projects/genius/

I also thank all the writers, poets, rebels, scientists, artists, and mad human beings who have influenced me.

This series is for you, so let's keep this going.

THANK YOU FOR READING THIS
FEIWEL AND FRIENDS BOOK

THE FRIENDS WHO MADE

GENIUS
the revolution

POSSIBLE ARE

JEAN FEIWEL,
Publisher

ALEXEI ESIKOFF,
Senior Managing Editor

LIZ SZABLA,
Associate Publisher

KIM WAYMER,
Senior Production Manager

RICH DEAS,
Senior Creative Director

ANNA POON,
Assistant Editor

HOLLY WEST,
Editor

EMILY SETTLE,
Administrative Assistant

ANNA ROBERTO,
Editor

LIZ DRESNER,
Associate Art Director

CHRISTINE BARCELLONA,
Editor

MELINDA ACKELL,
Copy Chief

KAT BRZOZOWSKI,
Editor

FOLLOW US ON FACEBOOK OR
VISIT US ONLINE AT MACKIDS.COM.

OUR BOOKS ARE FRIENDS FOR LIFE.